THE SHAKESPEARE
MURDERS

The following titles are all in the *Fonthill Complete A. G. Macdonell* Series.
The year indicates when the first edition was published.
See **www.fonthillmedia.com** for details.

Fiction

England, their England	(1933)
How Like an Angel	(1934)
Lords and Masters	(1936)
The Autobiography of a Cad	(1939)
Flight From a Lady	(1939)
Crew of the Anaconda (1940)	

Short Stories

The Spanish Pistol	(1939)

Non-Fiction

Napoleon and his Marshals	(1934)
A Visit to America	(1935)
My Scotland	(1937)

Crime and Thrillers written under the pseudonym of John Cameron

The Seven Stabs	(1929)
Body Found Stabbed	(1932)

Crime and Thrillers written under the pseudonym of Neil Gordon

The New Gun Runners	(1928)
The Factory on the Cliff	(1928)
The Professor's Poison	(1928)
The Silent Murders	(1929)
The Big Ben Alibi	(1930)
Murder in Earl's Court	(1931)
The Shakespeare Murders	(1933)

THE SHAKESPEARE MURDERS

MURDERS

A. G. MACDONELL

Originally published under the pseudonym of
NEIL GORDON

FONTHILL

Fonthill Media Limited

Fonthill Media LLC

www.fonthillmedia.com

office@fonthillmedia.com

First published 1933

This edition published in the United Kingdom 2012

British Library Cataloguing in Publication Data:

A catalogue record for this book is available from the British Library

Copyright © in Introduction, Fonthill Media 2012

ISBN 978-1-78155-021-2 (print)

ISBN 978-1-78155-112-7 (e-book)

Typeset in 11pt on 14pt Sabon

Printed and bound in England

Contents

Introduction to the 2012 Edition

The Shakespeare Murders is a classic of the A. G. Macdonell crime series, first published in 1933 at the height of the genre's popularity. It is one of several crime novels written by Macdonell under the pseudonym Neil Gordon.

Archibald Gordon Macdonell — Archie — was born on 3 November 1895 in Poona, India, the younger son of William Robert Macdonell of Mortlach, a prominent merchant in Bombay, and Alice Elizabeth, daughter of John Forbes White, classical scholar and patron of the arts. It seems likely that Archie was named after Brevet-Colonel A. G. Macdonell, CB, presumably an uncle, who commanded a force that defeated Sultan Muhammed Khan at the fort of Shabkader in the Afghan campaign of 1897.

The family left India in 1896 and Archie was brought up at 'Colcot' in Enfield, Middlesex, and the Macdonell family home of 'Bridgefield', Bridge of Don, Aberdeen. He was educated at Horris Hill preparatory school near Newbury, and Winchester College, where he won a scholarship. Archie left school in 1914, and two years later, he joined the Royal Field Artillery of the 51st Highland Division as a second lieutenant. His experiences fighting on the Western Front were to have a great influence on the rest of his life.

The 51st, known by the Germans as the 'Ladies from Hell' on account of their kilts, were a renowned force, boasting engagements at Beaumont-Hamel, Arras, and Cambrai. But by the time of the 1918 Spring Offensives, the division was war-worn and under strength; it suffered heavily and Archie Macdonell was invalided back to England, diagnosed with shell shock.

After the war, Macdonell worked with the Friends' Emergency and War Victims Relief Committee, a Quaker mission, on reconstruction in eastern Poland and famine in Russia. Between 1922 and 1927 he was on the headquarters staff of the League of Nations Union, which has prominent mention in *Flight from a Lady* and *Lords and Masters*. In the meantime he stood unsuccessfully as Liberal candidate for Lincoln in the general elections of 1923 and '24. On 31 August 1926, Macdonell married Mona Sabine Mann, daughter of the artist Harrington Mann and his wife, Florence Sabine Pasley. They had one daughter, Jennifer. It wasn't a happy marriage and they divorced in 1937, Mona citing her husband's adultery.

A. G. Macdonell began his career as an author in 1927 writing detective stories, sometimes under the pseudonyms Neil Gordon or John Cameron. He was also highly regarded at this time as a pugnacious and perceptive drama critic; he frequently contributed to the *London Mercury*, a literary journal founded in 1919 by John Collings Squire, the poet, writer, and journalist, and Archie's close friend.

By 1933 Macdonell had produced nine books, but it was only with the publication in that year of *England, Their England* that he truly established his reputation as an author. A gentle, affectionate satire of eccentric English customs and society, *England, Their England* was highly praised and won the prestigious James Tait Black Award in 1933. Macdonell capitalized on this success with another satire, *How Like an Angel* (1934), which parodied the 'bright young things' and the British legal system. The military history *Napoleon and his Marshals* (1934) signaled a new direction; although Macdonell thought it poorly rewarded financially, the book was admired by military experts, and it illustrated the range of his abilities. Between 1933 and 1941, A. G. Macdonell produced eleven more books, including the superlative *Lords and Masters* (1936), which tore into 1930s upper-class hypocrisy in a gripping and prescient thriller, and *The Autobiography of a Cad* (1939), an hilarious mock-memoir of one Edward Fox-Ingleby, ruthless landowner, unscrupulous politician, and consummate scoundrel.

The Shakespeare Murders was published in 1933, the same year that Macdonell achieved global recognition as a satirist with *England, Their England*. With unforgettable characters, particularly the gentleman-adventurer Peter Kerrigan, and an ingenious plot that keeps the reader guessing until the very end, it is an indulgent dip into the creative mind of a master crime writer at the peak of his form.

In 1940 Macdonell married his second wife, Rose Paul-Schiff, a Viennese whose family was connected with the banking firm of Warburg Schiff. His health had been weak since the First World War, and he died suddenly of heart failure in his Oxford home on 16 January 1941, at the age of 45.

A tall, athletic man with a close-cropped moustache, he was remembered as a complex individual, 'delightful ... but quarrelsome and choleric' by the writer Alec Waugh, who called him the Purple Scot, and by J. B. Morton, as 'a man of conviction, with a quick wit and enthusiasm and ... a sense of compassion for every kind of unhappiness.'

I

A Million Pounds

One fine spring morning Peter Kerrigan was strolling casually along the Euston Road in the direction of King's Cross. He saw a small man in a black felt hat coming towards him in a great hurry. The next moment a loiterer, who had been leaning against the rails and staring at the sky, lurched forward and bumped awkwardly into the small man and picked his pocket. Kerrigan, who took an interest in everything connected with his fellow-creatures, could not help admiring the dexterity with which the lounger had extracted the leather wallet and slipped it into his own coat pocket. The next moment Kerrigan himself bumped awkwardly into the lounger, neatly removed the stolen wallet and, after many profuse apologies, turned round and walked briskly after the little man in the black felt hat.

It was all done on the spur of the moment. There was no particular reason for going out of his way to befriend a total stranger, except that Kerrigan was in a mood of general benevolence towards mankind. It was a lovely morning; he had backed three winners the day before; the state of his exchequer was prosperous owing to an amazing run on the red at a select little club off Grosvenor Square a few weeks earlier; he was wearing a new suit; and there was no pastime he enjoyed so much as stealing from thieves. "It's not that I do it on high moral grounds," he used to explain, "but simply because thieves never prosecute."

So when he saw the unfortunate little man being robbed of his wallet, the temptation to recapture the swag was irresistible.

Whistling as gaily as any butcher's boy, Kerrigan marched along in the wake of the owner of the swag, and after they had turned a couple of corners he felt that it would be quite safe to examine the contents of the wallet. There was always a chance that it might contain a thousand pounds or the Koh-i-noor diamond; on the other hand, the seedy little man, who was in such a hurry, hardly looked the type that carries riches about with him.

The wallet contained no money, but only a miscellaneous collection of used-up railway tickets, bus tickets, a card of admission to the Reading-

Room of the British Museum made out in the name of Harrison Hone, a photograph or two, and a letter dated six weeks earlier. The words "a million pounds" caught Kerrigan's eye as he was about to put the letter back, and he immediately unfolded it and read it. It ran:

"Dear Harry, — This is written in great haste. A wonderful thing has happened to me, and before long I shall be worth at least a million pounds. You may hear strange things about me in the near future, but do not worry. I shall be all right, and when I have completed the transaction we will both be immensely rich men. And then what times we'll have. And what books we'll buy. And what drinks we'll drink. Give my love to Hilda and my nephews. — Yours affectionately,

JOHN.

"P.S. — 'Go, bid the soldiers shoot,' eh, old chap?"

Kerrigan whistled. "Worth a million pounds," he murmured. "This is a matter which needs investigating. I wonder why he wants the soldiers to shoot. Never mind, I'll find that out later."

He quickened his stride till he overtook the man in front, and then, bowing politely, he remarked, "Your wallet, sir, I think?"

The little man turned round and blinked rapidly at Kerrigan, and then at the wallet, and finally said, with a little stammer:

"Oh, thank you very much. Thank you very much indeed. Yes, it's mine. I must have dropped it. Thank you."

"Please don't mention it," replied Kerrigan affably, "I hope nothing of value has dropped out of it."

"There is nothing of value in it, I'm afraid," replied the other with a frank smile that Kerrigan rather liked. It converted the man's face in a moment from being nervous, harassed, and middle-aged into an almost schoolboyish simplicity and candour. The next moment the smile vanished from under the brown, straggly moustache, and the careworn expression came back. "But all the same," he went on, "I'm very grateful to you for your kindness." He put the wallet back into hi breast pocket, murmuring something about "wondering how on earth he had managed to do such a foolish thing," and then held out a thin, bony hand. Kerrigan had to think rapidly. Another instant, and it would have been the end of the interview. And he was interested in that million pounds. He glanced at his watch.

"What do you say to celebrating the recovery of your property with a little beer?" he inquired. "It is past half-past eleven; the taverns are open; a little judicious purchase of ale would harm neither of us, I fancy."

"Not for me, I thank you all the same," replied the other nervously. "The truth is, that I very rarely indulge in alcohol. Indeed I may say that I am practically a total abstainer."

"Very well. You drink milk and I'll support the Trade. Come on."

The little man hesitated and then said:

"Very well, sir. But it is only fair to tell you that I—er—unfortunately left all my money on the piano—"

"That's all right," said Kerrigan, "I'm full up to the ears with cash. Come along. I never ordered milk before in a tavern, but we live and learn. I wonder if they'll try to throw me out. It will be a novel experience."

He led his still hesitating companion into an adjacent public-house, and with a mixture of easy courtesy and familiarity accosted the brilliant damsel who presided at the counter.

"A very good morning to you, mademoiselle, and perhaps you would oblige me with a large can of ale and, if you stock such a commodity, a glass of milk. You stock it?"

"Yes, sir."

"Very well. A glass for my friend here, and," he lowered his voice, winked, and jerked his head almost imperceptibly towards his companion, "slip a spot of Jamaica into it."

The damsel was as experienced as she was brilliant, and Kerrigan convoyed his new friend to a table in the corner of the room and set down in front of him a large glass of rum and milk. The practically total abstainer took a large and hasty gulp at the milk and broke into a violent paroxysm of coughing which lasted for almost a minute. The brilliant lady laughed openly, and winked at Kerrigan, who returned the greeting with expert rapidity.

"What curious milk," the little man succeeded in saying at last, "it tastes all queer and hot."

"It's the Pasteur treatment," replied Kerrigan. "They use it in all public-houses nowadays."

"I had no idea of that," said the other doubtfully.

"I used to study Pasteurisation a good deal in the old days—"

"Oh, it's all changed since then," interrupted Kerrigan hastily. "This is the very latest thing."

"It certainly has an attractive taste. But I think it requires to be sipped rather than taken in draughts."

"That's right. Stick to sips and you can't go wrong. And now to business, Mr Hone."

"But—but—what business? And how do you know my name?" The little man looked round wildly. Possibly vague recollections of having read stories about people being decoyed into public-houses by strangers and then robbed and even murdered, flashed through his mind.

Kerrigan lowered his voice to a whisper. "Have you heard from John?"

Mr Hone started so abruptly that some of his Pasteurised milk was upset on the table.

"No," he replied, "I wish to God I had." Then he made a pathetic effort to pull himself together, and went on. "I'm afraid I don't know what you're talking about. And—er—if you don't mind, I think I'd better be moving on now. I'm in rather a hurry."

Peter Kerrigan assumed an air of portentous seriousness and said, "I'm on your side."

The little man gazed at him forlornly.

"Do you mean—" he began, and then stopped.

"Yes," replied Kerrigan, "I mean all that and a bit more. I know a good deal more about John than you think."

"Then do you know where he is now?" wailed Mr Hone. "He's been away for six weeks, and I'm getting so anxious about him."

"Six weeks! Is it as long as that? I shouldn't have thought it was more than four."

"It was six weeks yesterday."

"And not a word from him?"

"Not a word. Not a line. Not even a telegram." Kerrigan whistled.

"Not even a telegram. That's bad," he observed, shaking his head. "That's very bad."

"I'm so afraid he may have done something foolish," said Mr Hone in a despairing voice. "John was always the reckless one of the family. And when I got his letter—" He broke off again and peered suspiciously at Kerrigan.

The latter nodded reassuringly and said:

"The one about the million pounds. Yes, I know. Go on."

But Mr Hone was obviously very far from being reassured. The Pasteurised milk was mounting to his head, and was beginning to endow him with a fair amount of truculence. He looked rather like a mildly pugnacious rabbit.

"How do you know about it?" he demanded. "What do you know about it? Who are you, anyway? I don't even know your name."

"My name is Carkeek," replied Kerrigan without hesitation. "I am a private inquiry agent."

"But why should you inquire, even privately, into my brother's affairs?"

"Because I am representing an interested party," answered Mr Carkeek. "Some one," he added, "whose name I cannot divulge. But I can assure you it is a man of the very highest standing."

This puzzled Mr Hone, and his truculence gave way to a petulant bewilderment.

"It's all very mysterious," he announced, "and very tiresome. Six weeks ago I don't suppose there were two quieter or more placid lives being led in the whole of England than mine and my brother's. I was at work at my lectures, and he was at work in his library. And now my brother has vanished in search of a million pounds, and I'm all of a muddle. Do you know, Mr Carkeek," he concluded with desperate earnestness, "I'm even beginning to lose the thread of some of my lectures. Lectures, mind you, that I've been giving word for word for the last fifteen years. If it goes on like this, I shall be getting into trouble. Perhaps even getting the sack. And then where should I be, with a wife and two small boys to support?"

Kerrigan signed to the brilliant lady for another pair of drinks and answered cheerfully:

"Oh, you'll be able to support them on your share of the million pounds."

"I wish I knew what to do," murmured the little man with a wistful sigh. "I ought to do something, but I don't know what. I'm so—so unused to this sort of thing."

"Why not tell me the whole story?"

"There isn't anything to tell. My brother has vanished. And I don't know what to do about finding him. I don't even know if I ought to do anything. My brother is very peculiar. He is liable to fits of very bad temper. He is very unlike me in many ways."

"Where has your brother vanished from?"

"From where he was working."

"And where was that?"

But the rabbit was becoming pugnacious again. Mr Hone drained off his glass and stood up.

"I'm going now," he observed a trifle thickly. "Thank you very much for your hospitality. Your most kind hospitality—and your most kind return to me of my pocket-book. Greatly obliged to you, Mr Carkeek. Good-bye ol' fellow. Good-bye."

Kerrigan saw that nothing more was to be learnt about the disappearing brother and the million pounds, so he shook hands with the slightly inebriated lecturer, watched him depart a little unsteadily, and then followed him unobtrusively to a shabby house in the shabby lane off Gower Street, Bloomsbury, into which Mr Hone admitted himself with a fumbling latch-key.

II

Murder at the Manor

Peter Kerrigan was a young gentleman of about thirty-five who had lived by his wits since the early age of eleven. His father had been a good-looking, fascinating Irish waster, who had left Connemara for the good of Connemara late one night in a violent hurry, to the public annoyance and secret relief of the Royal Irish Constabulary which had always had a soft side for Terence Kerrigan. From Liverpool to Glasgow, and from Glasgow to New York, and from New York back to Hamburg, and from Hamburg to Petersburg, had been the outline of Terence Kerrigan's travels, until in about 1892 he married a beautiful Latvian girl and settled down to live in the neighbourhood of the docks of Riga. The result of the marriage was the one son, Peter, who played with the riff-raff of the waterside and learnt to swear fluently in twelve languages. Terence Kerrigan found vodka very much to his liking, and gradually discovered that he could live on a pennyworth of bread to an intolerable deal of it. His friends and acquaintances also discovered that vodka increased the natural fieriness of his Irish temper, and brawls became an everyday occurrence in the Irishman's life. Finally, when Peter was eleven years old, Terence and the beautiful Latvian Mrs Kerrigan were both killed in a violent stabbing affray in a dockside tavern in Riga. For the next eight years the lad supported himself, in various ways—some legal, some dubious, and some unquestionably illegal. On the outbreak of war, he happened to find himself in London and enlisted in an Irish infantry regiment. His peculiar talents and his fluency in languages, his repertoire of which had by now risen from twelve to eighteen, soon became so evident even to British Major-Generals (and if a thing is evident to a British Major-General it is probable that it is evident to other people as well) that he was transferred to the Intelligence Branch and dispatched to the fringe of Scandinavia nearest to Germany. From there he drifted to Russia, Siberia, Persia, Caucasia, Asia Minor, and Syria, and was the hero of many exploits and escapades, both creditable and discreditable, before the signature of the Peace Treaties sent him back to his civilian pursuits. By the time he was thirty-five he had acquired a very considerable knowledge of the ways of the world. He had learnt his way about the shady quarters of a good many large cities, and he collected an almost unequalled circle of shady acquaintances. If he had been given to boasting, which he was not, he could have boasted truthfully that he was personally known to a corrupt politician, a corrupt policeman, and a corrupt magistrate in three-quarters of the capitals of Europe. He was famous in the underworld of many countries for his open-handed generosity, his loyalty to friends, his versatile method of gaining a livelihood, his freelance independence of gangs, organisations, bosses, and vendettas, and he was universally respected for his remarkable skill in taking care of himself.

He was about five feet ten inches tall, with square shoulders and long arms; his hair was brown and curly and his eyes blue.

After following the nervous but stimulated lecturer to the house off Gower Street, Peter Kerrigan made a note of the address, hailed a taxi, and drove home to lunch. Home, at this period in the adventurer's career, was a flat in Grosvenor House; funds being plentiful, he was doing himself luxuriously. As he drove, and afterwards as he lunched, he considered the affairs of Mr Hone and his vanished brother. The question to be answered was, "Is it worthwhile following the matter up?" If Kerrigan had been hard up, he would not have dreamt of wasting five minutes over such a vague, nebulous business. But, situated as he was, with a comfortable nest-egg tucked away in the Grosvenor House branch of the Westminster Bank, and time being no object, it was just possible that a little diversion might be obtained from an investigation into the mysterious absence of the hot-tempered librarian. It all hinged on that phrase about the million pounds. Was it to be taken literally or was it a figure of speech? Did it mean, "I have a business deal on hand which will result in my netting the sum of one million golden sovereigns, which, carefully invested, will produce a yearly income of fifty thousand golden sovereigns?" Or did it mean, "I've a chance of making some money which will make me into a regular millionaire compared with what I've been making so far?" If the former was the correct version, then the matter was well worth investigating. Peter Kerrigan's ambition in life was to lay his fingers on a pile sufficiently large for him to be able to cut all the dubious and all the definitely illegal branches of his activities. And a good slice out of a million pounds would do the trick nicely.

But if the second version was correct, then the game was not worth twopence. Kerrigan had no idea of the amount of salary a librarian was likely to earn—he had, indeed, only the vaguest idea of what a librarian did, or why librarians existed at all—but he was fairly certain that a few hundreds would make a librarian feel like a millionaire. And he was not interested in hundreds. The librarian and his lecturing brother could keep them, so far as he was concerned. But a million! That was a very different story. By the time Kerrigan had reached the Stilton cheese, he had made up his mind to devote a day or two to the matter.

The first step was comparatively simple. At nine o'clock next morning, dressed in a shabby blue suit and an old bowler hat, and carrying a small brown handbag, he repaired to Gower Street and took up a post at the corner of that intellectual thoroughfare, and Mr Hone's dingy lane. His argument was that the lecturer must come out to deliver his lecture. He surely could not cram the people who listened to him—even if they only amounted to a handful—into the small house which he had let himself into the day before. Again, Kerrigan knew very little about lecturers and their habits, but he felt instinctively that they did not ply their trade in poky little houses in back streets. His instinct was right. At twenty minutes past nine Mr Hone came down the steps of his house. With one hand he clutched a large flat portfolio, with the other he tugged nervously at his straggly moustache. He looked even more careworn and harassed than on the day before. Kerrigan wondered if two glasses of rum and milk had given him a headache.

Mr Hone pattered past the watcher, keeping his eyes firmly fixed on the ground, and a few minutes later Kerrigan was ringing the bell of Number Twenty-seven. The lady of the house herself opened the door. She too bore unmistakably the marks of poverty and struggle. In happier circumstances she would have been comely, even pretty, but an incessant battle against adversity had made her careless of appearances. The mere task of living absorbed all her energies.

"Gas, Light, and Coke Company, madam," said Kerrigan briskly. "Meter inspection."

"Our meter was inspected yesterday," replied Mrs Hone, showing no disposition to admit the official.

"All the meters in this district were inspected yesterday," replied Kerrigan unabashed, "but there was a fire last night at our office, and all the records were lost. So we've got to do it all over again."

Mrs Hone gave way before this convincing explanation, coupled as it was with Kerrigan's most disarming smile, and pointed to the meter in the passage.

"Very well. There it is."

"We've also to inspect the gas-jets throughout the house, madam," went on the inspector. "There have been several cases of serious gas-poisoning lately, owing to faulty jets."

"Is that thrown in free, or do we have to pay extra for it?"

"Thrown in free, madam."

Mrs Hone's thin features relaxed into a faint smile as she said:

"Well, that's something anyway," and she stood back for Kerrigan to enter.

The only room in the house that was of the slightest interest was the small dining-room which obviously was used as day-nursery, study, and sitting-room as well. In one corner there was a small roll-top desk, and Kerrigan, during the couple of minutes in which he was left alone in the room, glanced hastily at the papers, letters, envelopes, and memoranda that lay upon it. One envelope immediately caught his eye, for it was written in the same shaky scrawl as the letter about the million pounds had been. The writing was quite unmistakable. Kerrigan stuffed the envelope in his pocket, and turned to examine the photographs on the mantelpiece. These consisted either of snapshots or of the ghastly family groups that were turned out with such pride by the photographers of twenty and thirty years ago. There was one that interested Peter, for it was obviously the wedding group of Mr, and Mrs Hone, and the best man was simply a larger edition of the bridegroom. As the same figure appeared in several other groups, and also in several of the snapshots, and as there was no other man except the lecturer himself, who appeared more than twice upon the mantelpiece, it was a fairly safe conclusion that the best man was brother John, the librarian, with his eyes upon a million pounds. Kerrigan added one of the snapshots to the envelope in his pocket, and, seeing nothing else that was likely to be of use to him, left the house.

As soon as he was well away from the neighbourhood of Gower Street, he pulled the envelope out of his pocket and examined the post-mark. It was Bicester, and the date, so far as he could decipher it, seemed to be about two months earlier. The writing interested him. It was shaky and straggly, and bore the unmistakable appearance of having been written by a very palsied hand. At the same time, it was the writing of an educated man. Here and there were letters which were beautifully formed, and the Greek "E's" and the bold capitals could never have been written by a product of the board schools.

"A literary gent who has taken to the bottle," was Kerrigan's verdict, as he carefully replaced the envelope in his pocket and signalled to a passing taxi.

"Did you ever hear of a town called Bicester?" he asked the driver.

"Yes, sir. Buckinghamshire. Can't drive you there, sir, without a fill-up of petrol."

"Can you drive me to the station that would take me there?"

"Yes, sir. Paddington."

"Paddington it is then. And first drift round to Grosvenor House so that I can get the ancestral tails and topper."

Peter Kerrigan's knowledge of England was almost exclusively confined to London and one or two of the seaports. The rural Midlands were something quite new to him, and he sat in the corner of his carriage, entranced by the endless succession of green meadows, flower-laden hedges, and leafy woods. It was so peaceful and undisturbed, so utterly different to the swift, hard, ruthless kaleidoscope of men and women and events that he was accustomed to.

But as the miles were reeled off and, according to the map on the carriage wall, the train was rapidly approaching Bicester, Kerrigan began to get puzzled. There was no change in the quiet countryside. It was still meadows and woods and isolated cottages. At any moment he expected that the train would plunge into a seething, swarming, black industrial area. And he kept on hoping that it would. For this rural placidity was not the sort of surroundings in which a million pounds could be picked up, nor was it the sort of place in which business men would be likely to gather to plan vast secret coups of finance. "You couldn't be secret in a country like this," he reflected, "everyone knows where everyone else is, and what every one else is doing."

And when the train drew up at the almost deserted platform of Bicester Station, and Peter got out and gazed at the sleepy little town shimmering in the midday heat, he felt half inclined to take the next train back to London. Either it was a pure chance that the letter had been posted at Bicester, on a weekend visit, perhaps, or on a holiday—or else the librarian had not meant more than a few pounds when he so glibly and impressively used the word "million."

But as it was nearly lunchtime and no trains to London were due to arrive for a couple of hours, he decided to stroll into the town, look round, have lunch, show the snapshot to one or two people on the chance of a lucky recognition, and then if nothing had happened, to return quietly in the afternoon.

A citizen of the town directed him to the Angel Hotel, as being a suitable place for a gentleman to obtain a meal, and Peter Kerrigan strolled, hands in pockets, in that direction. It was a warm, drowsy day, and Bicester seemed to be rather a drowsy place. But Kerrigan found it extremely interesting.

It was quite unlike anything he had met in England before. It was so sleepy and so placid, and yet at the same time so quietly prosperous in appearance. Nothing had ever happened here and nothing ever would happen here. That was the impression he got. As for picking up a million pounds, it was even more fantastic than it had seemed in the train. Kerrigan smiled at the thought of the wild-goose chase that had brought him down to the heart of rural England in search of financial adventure and profit, and the next moment he turned in to the lounge of the Angel Hotel.

After a few preliminary exchanges on the subject of the crops, the past hunting season, and the prospects of the next hunting season, with the landlord, Kerrigan asked casually:

"Did you ever meet a man in these parts called Hone?"

The landlord looked at him queerly and replied: "Yes, I did meet a man called Hone, and I should like to meet him again. He owes me three pounds fourteen shillings, and I've about as much chance of ever seeing that money as I have of flying to the moon."

"Is that the man?" asked Kerrigan, producing the photograph.

"That's the man," replied the landlord after a brief scrutiny. Then he looked at Kerrigan knowingly and winked. "I'll lay six to four that I can guess your profession, sir, if you give me three shots."

"I'll take you in sixpences," said Kerrigan, who could never resist a bet.

The landlord leant across the bar and said in a loud stage whisper, "Bailiff or Detective or Solicitor." Peter Kerrigan saw that he had stumbled on a piece of luck which ought to be followed up, and he solemnly laid a florin upon the counter.

"You win," he remarked, "and allow me to tell you that you're a pretty shrewd chap."

"Pretty shrewd, pretty shrewd," exclaimed the triumphant landlord. "And which of the three are you, sir?"

"Ah! Now you're asking," parried Kerrigan with a laugh; "but I'll tell you this. If you help me to find Hone, I'll help you to get your three pounds fourteen shillings back."

"Come right in," said the landlord, opening the door of his private room.

"This Mr Hone," he proceeded, when they were comfortably installed in arm-chairs, "had some sort of job at the big house here—"

"Whose big house?"

"Lord Claydon's place, outside Bicester. You've heard of Lord Claydon's place? It's called Marsh Manor. Never heard of it? Well, you do surprise me! It's a couple of miles out, on the way to Aylesbury. It's the biggest place in the district. This man Hone worked there—sort of secretary, I suppose."

"Librarian, perhaps."

"It might have been. He looked a learned sort of fellow in some ways. Wore spectacles and always had a book under his arm. But mind you, in other ways he looked like a wrong 'un. Drank a lot of whisky—that's what he owes the money for—and had a look about the eyes as if he'd been at it for some time. Man of fifty or thereabouts. Shifty expression on his face, if you know what I mean. Still, he was a good customer. That's why I gave him the credit. And now he's skipped out and owes me three pounds fourteen. A real wrong 'un, that's what he's turned out."

"Do you know why he left?"

"Not an idea."

"How long was he there?"

"About eighteen months, I should say."

"Have they got a new man in his place?" inquired Kerrigan.

"I'm told so. But I've not seen him."

"Do you happen to know anything about Hone? I mean, what his plans were, or what he was likely to turn to after he left here?"

"No. He wasn't a talkative man, even when he'd had a few drinks."

Kerrigan pondered. The landlord did not seem to know very much that was of use, except the one fact that Hone had worked for Lord Claydon. A visit to Marsh Manor seemed to be the next move. The landlord assured him that Lord Claydon was at home, and was entertaining a party of friends; he also informed Kerrigan that he himself was the owner of a car which he hired out at very moderate charges, and that the hotel had accommodation also at a very moderate rate in the event of the young detective (or bailiff or solicitor) wishing to stay the night.

Kerrigan accepted both car and accommodation, and in a few minutes was driving himself out towards Marsh Manor in an ancient and rattly Ford.

It was impossible to miss the entrance to the Manor. A wide semicircle of iron gates was supported on massive pillars of grey stone and surmounted by a huge coat-of-arms, also in grey stone, while an ancient half-timbered lodge was hidden behind a couple of gigantic plane trees. The avenue ran through a grass park for half a mile and then vanished into an impenetrable screen of woods. The Manor itself was invisible from the road and only a thin column of smoke, ascending into the air above the trees, showed that a house was there at all.

Peter Kerrigan drove boldly through the imposing gateway, quite unawed by its magnificence, and rattled and clanked up to the front door of the Manor, a large, square, yellow Georgian building. As he drew up with a piercing shriek from the brakes of the car, he got an unpleasant surprise which made him hastily alter his plans. He had intended to announce himself as a detective from Scotland Yard, but when he saw a policeman standing on the top of the steps which led up to the door, he decided that this would be a little indiscreet. He therefore hastily adjusted his outlook to that of a solicitor, tried to assume a portentously solemn appearance, and dismounted from the car. The policeman eyed his approach coldly and, on the top step, interposed his massive person between Kerrigan and the front door, and inquired his business.

"I am a solicitor," began the young man smoothly, "and I wish to speak to Lord Claydon for a minute or two."

"If you will give me your card, sir, I will take it in." Kerrigan, who never travelled without a varied supply of calling-cards to meet varied emergencies, produced one on which was printed "Mr Algernon Phipps, Y201 Albany, London, W.1. Almack's, Bucks, Boodles." It was not the card he would have selected for a family solicitor, but he had been taken unawares, and the production of half a dozen cards and the selection of a suitable one would have aroused a certain amount of justifiable suspicion.

The policeman examined it and then handed it to another policeman who was stationed in the hall. Kerrigan was longing to know what they were doing at the Manor, but decided not to risk a direct question. Policemen were apt to resent direct questions.

The next moment the last man in England that he wanted to see came out of the house, holding the card in his hand. It was Inspector Fleming, of Scotland Yard, and he and Inspector Fleming had known each other for a good many years.

The Inspector smiled and held out a hand.

"Hullo, Kerrigan," he said. "Just the sort of place you would go and turn up in. Half a moment." He turned to the policeman. "Where's this man Phipps?" he asked.

"There he is, sir."

"Excuse me," intervened Kerrigan blandly, looking over Fleming's shoulder at the card. "There is a misunderstanding. I see that I have by mistake sent in the wrong card. How foolish of me!"

"What's the game this time, my lad?" asked the detective with another smile.

"He said he was a solicitor, sir," put in the policeman with an aggrieved air. He felt that somehow or other he had been "put upon" by the plausible stranger.

"When you know this gentleman as well as I do," replied Fleming, "you'll know that he's capable of saying anything. Come inside, Kerrigan; I want a word with you." He led the way into a large hall and drew the young man across to a sofa. "What are you doing here?" he asked. "I've got a very special reason for wanting to know."

"I'll tell you the truth, Fleming," replied Kerrigan after a moment's hesitation, "and the truth isn't a thing I would tell to everyone."

"No, I'm sure of that," put in Fleming dryly.

"Come, come, laddie, none of that. Just concentrate on listening for a bit. I came down here to discover the whereabouts of a certain Mr John Hone, until six weeks ago librarian to the gent who owns this shack."

"And why did you want to know his whereabouts?"

Again Kerrigan hesitated and finally he said:

"I heard from his brother that he thought he was likely to make a large sum of money in the near future."

"How?"

"Ah! That's just what I wanted to know."

"You had no idea, Kerrigan?"

"Straight, I hadn't."

"I see. And is that all you can tell me?"

"Absolutely all, Fleming. As a matter of fact, I wouldn't have worried about the thing at all, because I'd got such vague information to go on, only it happens that I've got plenty of leisure just now and I thought I might glance at it."

"I see. And how did you propose setting about finding Mr John Hone?"

"I intended to ask old Lord What's-his-name, the lad who owns the spot. I thought he might know something. And I thought I might try to have a word with the new librarian, if there is such a party."

"There was such a party until last night," replied Fleming.

Kerrigan got excited.

"You don't mean to tell me that another of them has skipped out?" he said.

"Not skipped out," said the Inspector. "Murdered. The librarian was murdered in the library some time during the night."

III

The Treasure

"One librarian talks about a million pounds and vanishes," murmured Fleming thoughtfully, "and his successor is murdered."

"I had no idea it was such an exciting trade," Kerrigan observed, but the detective paid no attention to him. He was staring at the carpet and frowning. Kerrigan waited. At last Fleming looked up with a grin.

"The last time you and I met professionally," he remarked, "was in the matter of that murder in Earls Court and the North of England forgers."

"That's right."

"As a direct result of your being allowed to do what you liked, the boss of the forgers got clear away with his life and liberty, and you got clear away with a whole sack of forged pound-notes. By the way, how did you manage to get them changed?"

Kerrigan winked.

"I suppose that's the reason for your having so much leisure," went on Fleming. "How many notes were there in that sack?"

"You don't suppose, do you," said the young man, "that if you can't collect any evidence against me, I'm going to manufacture it myself?" He glanced round, and lowered his voice. "As a matter of fact, there were four thousand five hundred and twenty-nine."

"Quite so," replied Fleming. "A tidy little sum. And now look here, Master Kerrigan, this time you're not going to be allowed to operate outside, on your own, like you did before. You're inside, and you stay inside, where I can keep an eye on you. Do you understand?"

"Perfectly. And what's more, I'll make a bargain with you. I'll help you to find the murderer, if you promise to leave me the million if I get hold of it. Is it a deal?"

"Most certainly not," replied Fleming firmly. "But I rely on you, as a law-abiding citizen, to bring me any information which you think may be of use."

"That's all jolly fine," retorted Kerrigan, "but how do I know what may be of use until you tell me all about the murder? Come on, Colonel, shoot the story."

After a moment's thought, Fleming said:

"I don't see why not. As a matter of fact there isn't much to tell so far. The librarian was a man of about thirty, called Walter Newman, of Canadian origin; he was brought up in America and subsequently came to this country. He was taken on here to fill the vacancy caused by Hone's departure about six weeks ago; he had very high recommendations from several people in Canada, and one or two in England. Lord Claydon took him on at once, because he is anxious to get the catalogue of the library finished as soon as possible. It's an enormous library, and it's never been properly catalogued, apparently."

"Is it worth a million pounds?" inquired Kerrigan. "I don't know much about these things."

"It's supposed to be worth about ten thousand pounds. But of course, when it's all catalogued, it may turn out to be worth more."

"Or less."

"Exactly. But the library isn't the valuable thing about this place, Kerrigan. The library's a bagatelle compared to the Treasure."

Kerrigan was thrilled by the word. It conjured up visions of everything that he had been pursuing for years—gold, silver, jewels, anything which could be converted into wealth, luxury, and ease.

"Treasure?" he repeated in a reverent whisper.

"Yes. There's no secret about it. It used to be quite a well-known story."

"Go on," said Kerrigan. "It's not well-known to me. I've never heard of it."

"In about 1830," said Fleming, "there was a mad Lord Claydon who brought it back from India. He was an art-collector; collected anything he could lay his hands on—pictures, books, furniture, jewels, carpets, tapestries, sculpture, anything. The house is full of stuff he brought home from his travels. And, incidentally, there is a tremendous lot of valuable stuff in the house. But the most valuable of the lot, according to himself, was the Treasure which he brought back from India on his last voyage. He got a great iron safe made for it in one of the cellars and a huge iron double door for the cellar itself, and then he went and died, and the Treasure has never been seen from that day to this."

"What! It wasn't in the safe?"

"It wasn't anywhere. There's been about a hundred years of searching for it, but in the last twenty or thirty years they've rather given it up as a bad job. They're very doubtful, in fact, if it ever existed. You see, the old chap was as mad as a hatter from all accounts."

"And what did the Treasure consist of?"

"Ah! That's one of the points. Nobody ever saw it. The old boy came home in a great state of excitement and announced that he'd got the greatest treasure of his life, and chucked every soul out of the house except a pair of Hindu servants whom he'd brought back with him. After a couple of months he threw open the house again, and got the safe made, and he told his eldest son—the present man's grandfather that he would tell him about the Treasure when he was on his death-bed. And a week later he broke his neck hunting, and that was the end of him, and his bag of diamonds or whatever it was."

Peter Kerrigan whistled.

"And now Librarian John Hone has found them, eh?"

Fleming sat up.

"I wonder. But why kill his successor? That seems rather a difficulty."

"Yes. It does. By the way, how was he killed?"

"Hit on the head with a poker—the devil of a hard bit."

"And is that all the story so far?"

"That's all," said Fleming, getting up. "Turn your active and shockingly experienced mind on to the problem, my lad, and keep your eyes open. Let me know if anything occurs to you and don't try any monkey-tricks or you'll find yourself in Queer Street. By the way, you might have a look at the house-party and let me know what you think of them. They're an odd crew, so far as I've been able to make out. But I haven't had long enough to give them a real look over."

"You can't give me any assurance about my share in any swag that emerges?" began Kerrigan, but Fleming cut him short.

"No, I can't," he replied, "and I wouldn't if I could. Now come and be introduced to Lord Claydon. By the way, I wonder what you'd better be? I don't want him to think you're helping me."

"I'm going to help myself," murmured Kerrigan, but not loud enough for the detective to hear. In a louder voice he said:

"I'll be agent of the Insurance Company that the librarian fellow was insured with. How about that?"

"It'll do. But you don't look like an insurance agent. You're too well dressed. However, nobody will pay much attention to you," and Fleming led the way into a billiard-room at the end of a long corridor.

"Oh, won't they?" said Kerrigan to himself, as he saw a couple of girls talking in a far corner of the room. "Just you wait, my lad!"

The next moment he was being introduced to Lord Claydon as the representative of the Moon Life Insurance Company of Canada. Lord Claydon, a middle-aged man of about fifty-five, bowed coldly and said nothing. He obviously did not like insurance agents. He obviously liked them even less when Fleming explained that it was essential that this one should stay in the house until the inquiry was over. Lord Claydon turned abruptly and called to one of the girls in the corner:

"Pamela, here's a—a—gentleman from the insurance people who has to be put up. Will you fix a room for him, and—er—look after him." And without waiting for an answer, his lordship turned away, and walked across to the fireplace where another middle-aged man was standing, and plunged into conversation with him. Fleming slipped out and went back to work. The girl addressed as Pamela walked slowly round the billiard-table and nodded unsmilingly to the representative of the insurance company.

"How d'you do? I'll tell Perkins to arrange something for you. It'll face north, though. But it can't be helped." She nodded again and went back to her corner.

Kerrigan was left isolated in the middle of the room. He looked at the fireplace, at the two middle-aged men, and then he looked at the corner where the two girls were engaged in earnest talk with a tall, thin young man, and decided to plunge into the latter group. He approached them with easy confidence, undaunted by the frigid silence which greeted his advance.

"Tiresome things, these murders," he observed genially. "Upset the domestic staff always, what?"

"Yes," replied the girl Pamela. She was a tall, good-looking girl of about twenty-three or four, beautifully dressed and manicured, with marcel-waved black hair and crimson lips, thin eyebrows, and unfathomable depths of self-confidence.

"I suppose the next thing is to spot the murderer," proceeded Kerrigan. "Do you think it's an outside job or an inside job?"

"I don't know," said Pamela.

"And what do you think, sir?" he addressed the thin young man.

"I don't know," replied the thin young man. Peter Kerrigan glanced swiftly over him and was interested in his appearance. His face was very brown and he had a scar across one of his cheeks as if he had once been the hero of a German student-duel, and he looked very competent. His hair was dark brown, his eyes were light brown, and an upturned moustache gave him a distinguished appearance. His manner, to put it mildly, was stand-offish. Kerrigan turned to the other girl and was even more interested. She was very tall—only an inch or so short of six feet—and she carried herself magnificently. An exquisite pink-and-white natural complexion was emphasised by contrast with a superb mass of dark red hair that glowed with dull splendour in the sunlight, and there was something about her face that made Kerrigan think that she might have a sense of humour, in spite of the statuesque coldness with which she was regarding him.

"I must introduce myself," he said, with a comprehensive bow to the trio. "My name is Kerrigan. Peter Kerrigan."

The girl called Pamela obviously felt that some sort of show of civility was called for, and she said in a perfunctory way:

"Miss Shackleford. Captain Streatfield—let me introduce—"

They both bowed distantly.

"What about you, Miss Shackleford?" Kerrigan persevered. "Have you any theories about the murder?"

"None, I'm afraid."

Kerrigan felt like taking out his handkerchief and mopping his brow. He had never known such uphill work. Instead, he tried a new tack.

"What about the famous Treasure, eh? This business brings it into the sphere of practical politics again, all right. I bet that librarian knew a thing or two about it."

There was no answer from the trio, and Peter became aware that Lord Claydon and the other man by the fireplace were listening. The next moment the door opened and a short, tubby, cheerful-looking man came in. With almost audible sighs of relief the silent party in the corner broke up and went eagerly to meet him.

"Come and make up a four, Mr Rubin," cried Lady Pamela. "We've been waiting for you."

"I could not get away a moment sooner," replied the newcomer in a strong American accent. "I have been making a deposition to the cops, and it took them thirty minutes to write down in quadruplicate that I was asleep last night from eleven-fifteen till seven-forty this morning, and heard no sounds or signs of the dastardly crime."

A card-table was put out and the four sat down to bridge. Kerrigan strolled across to the fireplace, and the other man was introduced as Sir George Ilford. Sir George was the only one of the party who seemed disposed to talk. He was about six feet five, and his breadth of shoulder, his bushy black eyebrows, and his heavy black moustache added to the formidable aggressiveness of his whole appearance.

"Insurance, are you?" he said, staring down at Kerrigan. "Come to dispute the claim, I suppose. That's all you fellows ever do. You don't look like an insurance tout, either. But all you insurance chaps get prosperous on the mugs who pay the premiums." Peter Kerrigan looked up at him coolly.

"You don't look like a mug," he observed. The big man was surprised at this answer, and could not think of any better reply than, "You're right there."

The conversation got no farther; Lord Claydon looked at his watch and said nervously to Ilford something about a stroll in the rose-garden before tea, and the two men went out of one of the French windows, the host pausing to say, "I hope you'll make yourself at home, Mr—er—" before he went out.

"I'm not being what you might call a social success," thought Kerrigan, as he strolled out of the billiard-room to make a survey of the house. "They don't seem to cotton on to me as a guest very much."

Seeing a telephone in the hall, he rang up his hotel in London to ask for a bag to be packed and dispatched to Marsh Manor by passenger train, and then he wandered round the house.

"There are two possible hypotheses," he said to himself, as he strolled slowly along one of the corridors which seemed to abound in the vast mansion. "Either the Treasure is still here, or it was taken away last night. John Hone may have got wind of its hiding-place or he may not. But if he did, I'll swear he didn't take it away with him. Because there would be no point in killing the lad last night if the stuff had already gone."

"I wish Fleming trusted me," was his next reflection, and he heaved a deep sigh as he admitted that there was no particular reason for the Inspector to trust him. It was pretty annoying, though, to think that there was a very good chance that an immensely valuable treasure was lying somewhere in the house, and that if anyone found it, it would probably be the police officials themselves.

A distant gong seemed to indicate that tea was ready, but Kerrigan decided to continue his stroll; and after an hour of methodical pacing, of counting yards and door-handles, of ascending and descending staircases, and of comparing his results with a plan of the house which he found on the wall of the gun-room, he was able to reach a fairly accurate mental picture of the lie of the land. The ground-floor was enormous, the first floor much smaller, and the jumble of attics on the second floor was about the same size as the first. But almost all the activity of the house was on the ground-floor, which included sixteen out of the thirty bedrooms. The library was separate from the rest of the house and was connected with it by a glass-roofed passage. From the date on the gun-room plan, it was fairly certain that the mad Lord Claydon had built the library, and from the scale of the plan it was obvious that it was an extremely large room. But close study of it was impossible at the moment, owing to the presence in the glass-roofed passage of an exceptionally bulky and taciturn policeman with instructions to let no one pass.

Another bulky and taciturn policeman was on duty at the top of the cellar stairs, so there was no opportunity of examining the famous safe which had not contained the Treasure; and Peter, having discovered his allotted bedroom on the first floor, retired to consider the recent form of the horses who were due to race against each other in the Derby on the following Wednesday week. At half-past six a footman of stately demeanour appeared and announced coldly that he had come to lay out his evening clothes, and was palpably shaken on hearing that the gentleman had brought no evening clothes, or indeed any luggage at all. He had a poor opinion at any time of gentlemen visitors who were relegated to the first floor, facing north; and a visitor who addressed him as "old fish" was little better than a social pariah. Alfred indicated his opinion by a superior lift of his eyebrows which Kerrigan did not miss. He immediately counter-attacked.

"Is there a telephone on this floor?" he demanded. "There are six telephones on this floor," replied Alfred loftily.

"Then get me the Duke of Westminster at once."

"The Duke of—" faltered Alfred, his nerve beginning to give way.

"Of Westminster. And please be kind enough to bring me a whisky and soda."

"Yes, sir. Very good, sir. At once, sir," replied the footman, almost backing out of the room in mingled deference and alarm. He returned in two minutes with a large whisky and soda, and in five minutes with the information that His Grace was in the south of France. This did not surprise Kerrigan, who had read the news of His Grace's departure in the *Daily Mail* that morning, but he remarked petulantly, "Dash the man! He might have told me." Alfred bowed deeply and retired. At seven o'clock he returned to say that the Inspector of Police wished him to attend in the library, and Kerrigan went down eagerly to the scene of the crime.

The library was shaped like the nave of a Gothic church. It was enormously long and enormously high, with a vaulted roof. The books were crammed into bookcases about twelve feet high—the upper shelves being accessible only from step ladders which were scattered about the room, and there seemed to be thousands of them. High above these shelves there was a narrow gallery, running round all four sides of the library, and reached by a spiral staircase at each end. The floor was crowded with tables on which lay glass cases, and there was one large table covered with papers. At the far end there was a small room which was used as the librarian's office; it had no door communicating with the outside, and so formed a kind of cul-de-sac.

Kerrigan found Fleming giving instructions to his sergeant, who was scribbling in a notebook. The Inspector beckoned him in.

"This is the place, Kerrigan. And under that sheet is the—er—chief exhibit. I want you to have a look at it, in a moment. In the meantime, what do you think of the house party?"

"A genial crowd, a genial crowd," replied Kerrigan. "One of them very nearly spoke a civil word to me, and another one almost recognised my existence when I addressed her."

"Streatfield and Lady Pamela are engaged to be married."

"Then I'm sorry for both of them," said Kerrigan wholeheartedly.

Fleming took him by the lapel of his coat and led him into a corner.

"Look here, my lad," he said in an undertone, "I can't make you help me if you don't want to. But if you're after this Treasure, your way lies along my way for a considerable extent, and we might do worse than pool our information."

"All right," said Kerrigan. "Pool away; you begin."

"Well, the first thing," said Fleming, "is that this murder was unpremeditated."

"And the man was bashed with a poker?"

"Yes. The library poker."

"That means that who ever did it was pretty quick, and pretty desperate."

"Yes," agreed Fleming, "and I'll show you one of the things that made him quick."

He opened a cardboard box and displayed an automatic pistol.

"This was in the librarian's hand," he said. "A queer thing for a librarian to have, eh?"

"May I look at it?" asked Kerrigan, stretching out his hand. "You've got all the finger-prints, and what not, off it?"

Fleming nodded.

"American—1930 make—not fired lately—common as flies in Chicago—no sort of help there," murmured Kerrigan as he made a rapid and expert survey of the weapon.

"He had two spare clips of cartridges in his coat-pocket and two more in his kit upstairs. And he carried it under his arm."

"Whew! He must have been one of the lads! That's Al Capone stuff."

"Yes, I thought that too," agreed Fleming. But apart from the gun there wasn't anything else at all suspicious in his outfit. Come along and have a look at him."

The dead librarian had been killed outright with a single smashing blow of the poker on the side of the head. Kerrigan looked at the body, which was clad in dressing-gown, pyjamas, and bedroom slippers, for several minutes before he said:

"The hands might be the hands of a man who never did any manual labour, but spent all his time pottering about with books; they might also be the hands of a man who played the piano, or mended watches, or opened safes."

"Opened safes?" said Fleming sharply.

Kerrigan spread out his own thin, beautifully-shaped fingers.

"Like mine," he remarked blandly.

There was a silence for a moment, and then Kerrigan glanced at the inside of the dead man's bedroom slippers.

"American make," he murmured.

"Yes. Cincinnati. The man was a Canadian who had lived in the States."

"If I were you, Fleming, I would go into those references of his. I can't believe that librarians in this dead-and-alive corner of a law-abiding country carry guns under their arms."

"I have already wired about them." Kerrigan patted the Inspector on the back.

"You are coming on, my boy. I shall recommend you to the Commissioners for promotion."

"Any more cheek," replied Fleming with a laugh, "and I shall recommend you to the magistrates for deportation."

"In the meantime, what's the next move?" Fleming lowered his voice again.

"Watch the house-party. It was an inside job."

Kerrigan whistled. "Are you sure?"

"Absolutely."

"One of the house-party?"

"Or one of the servants. Maitland—my sergeant—is going to watch the servants' hall. You and I will take the rest."

The gong sounded again from the house, and the policeman on duty at the door of the library put his head in and said, "Dinner is announced, sir."

"One more word," said Kerrigan. "Is there any trace of anything having been taken away from here during the night?"

Fleming laughed.

"If there were a million golden sovereigns hidden here, then I can assure you they have not been removed. But if there was a handful of jewels, then nobody can possibly say whether they have been removed or not. In any case, I don't think they are likely to have left the house."

IV

Sparring for Position

The short and tubby Mr Rubin proved to be the life and soul of the dinner-party. He chattered away gaily in his high-pitched American voice, and did not seem to mind in the least that the only people at the table who paid the slightest attention to him were Kerrigan and a guest whom the latter was only meeting for the first time. This was an elderly gentleman called Tollemache, a small, bent, scholarly-looking individual with gold-rimmed spectacles and grey hair, and a courteous, old-world manner in which he apologised frequently for allowing his attention to stray from the topics under discussion. It transpired in the course of some skilfully veiled questioning by Kerrigan, that Mr Tollemache was an expert valuer of works of art, who was apparently doing for the art-treasures of Marsh Manor what the unfortunate librarian had been doing for the library.

The indefatigably gay Mr Rubin, disregarding most courageously the damping atmosphere of the dinner-table, persisted in chaffing Mr Tollemache on the chances that he might provide the next victim for the murderer.

"Art-valuers for art's sake," he kept on repeating waggishly, till poor little Mr Tollemache positively squirmed in his chair, and the magnificent Miss Shackleford finally came to his rescue.

"I think we ought to change the subject," she announced coldly, but decisively.

"I cordially agree," exclaimed Kerrigan, and his quick eye noticed that the girl looked as if his support made her sorry that she had spoken.

"Very well," said Mr Rubin. "Let's talk about Insurance. I understand that this gentleman represents an Insurance Company. Will you quote me a risk for a wet day for the Derby?"

"Three and a tenth," replied Peter glibly; he had not the faintest idea of the technical jargon of the profession he was representing.

Sir George Ilford looked sharply down the table from under his heavy black eyebrows.

"Three and a tenth what?" he inquired in a waspish tone that did not sound at all friendly.

"Oh, just three and a tenth," replied Kerrigan airily. "That's the market figure."

Captain Streatfield took a hand in the talk.

"How do you fellows work out a figure like that? It's all Greek to me."

"We employ a staff of highly-trained meteorologists who calculate the secondary arterial depressions," answered the insurance agent, "and their results are passed on to the staff of chemico-mathematicians who reduce the whole thing to a common denominator and recommend a figure which goes before the next board-meeting." "And if that doesn't choke 'em off," thought Kerrigan, "I'll eat my hat."

Streatfield's face had gone completely blank as he nodded vaguely several times, but little Mr Tollemache became quite excited.

"But what—what is a secondary, arterial depression?" he cried. "I've been an amateur meteorologist for years, and I've never heard of such a thing. Will you explain it to me?"

"Damn it!" thought Kerrigan, "that's hard luck!" Aloud he replied:

"Explain it, my dear sir? I'll do better than that. I'll send you a book about it, and, if I may, a little pamphlet of my own on the subject. Don't let me forget to do that. Give me your card after dinner. And what is your fancy for the Derby, Mr Rubin?" he went on hastily to avoid the possible importunities of the amateur meteorologist. In this he was successful, for the discussion of various likely winners of the Derby almost made the conversation general. Kerrigan, during the exchange of certainties and tips and likely winners, glanced swiftly round the table. There was no doubt that an atmosphere of tension existed in Marsh Manor; an atmosphere not entirely to be accounted for by the tragic occurrence of the night before. The librarian had only been among them for a few weeks, and Sir George Ilford and Lord Claydon and the tough but pleasant-looking captain did not seem to be the sort of men who would be unduly cast down by the death, even the violent death, of a comparative stranger. Lord Claydon himself was nervous and silent. Dark lines under his eyes, a tremulous wrist when he lifted his wine-glass, a hunted expression, combined to give him an air of worry and depression. Kerrigan caught him several times staring at Sir George Ilford with a curious, unfathomable look in his eyes, and each time he started perceptibly on realising that Kerrigan was watching him.

After dinner the two girls and Streatfield and Rubin returned to their bridge-table; Mr Tollemache dived into an Art Quarterly, Lord Claydon disappeared, and the dark and immense baronet challenged Kerrigan to a game of picquet.

On the delivery of the challenge, Streatfield looked up sharply from the card-table and started to say something, but was checked by Miss Shackleford's quick interruption of "Your deal, David."

Kerrigan soon discovered that Ilford was a fairly good picquet-player, and by dint of carefully masking his own expertness, succeeded in losing fourteen pounds in an hour without arousing any suspicion. The result was exactly as he had hoped. The baronet grew exceedingly cheerful; several whiskies and sodas were sent for and consumed; and at the end of another hour's play, Sir George, twenty-three pounds up, was positively mellow. By this time they were alone in the drawing-room—Mr Tollemache having retired to bed and the other four to play snooker—and Ilford became almost confidential.

"Who did the murder, Mr What's-your-name?" he asked. And without waiting for an answer he went straight on, "What do you make of Rubin, eh?"

"A very nice gentleman, I think," said Kerrigan, assuming a simple expression, as of one who was anxious to please everybody.

"Oh, you do, do you?" replied Ilford truculently. "Well, you're easy to please. And what's he doing here, eh?"

"He's a guest of his lordship's, I suppose."

"A queer sort of guest," said the other with a frown. "Came here a week ago with a letter of introduction from Claydon's son in New York, was asked to stay to dinner, and has been here ever since and shows no signs of going. What do you make of that, Mr Insurance Tout?"

"It means that his lordship is a very hospitable man, surely."

"It means also that Mr Rubin wants investigating, as I told that inspector this morning. I'll tell you what happened, of course. Young Marsh, Claydon's son, is out in New York running after some damned chorus girl or other, as he always is, and he must have met Rubin and told him all about the Treasure. Sort of thing Marsh would do when he'd got a couple of drinks inside him. And Rubin has come over to try and get it for himself. The question is whether he got it or not—last night."

Kerrigan did his best to give a start of horror, but felt that it was unconvincing. Ilford, however, did not seem to notice anything, for he went on:

"That shakes you a bit, doesn't it? What do you think, eh? Does Mr Rubin look the sort of man that murders an unfortunate young librarian in cold blood?"

"Oh, I—I—don't know anything about that sort of thing," replied Kerrigan, achieving a very passable stutter of alarm.

The baronet sneered.

"The place is full of queer guests," he said. "But then, it's a queer world nowadays. I never thought I'd see the day when I'd be glad to sit down to picquet with an insurance tout. Never mind. Your money is as good as anyone else's. At least I hope your cheque is. Have another drink. I'm going to bed. We must have another game tomorrow night," and he stalked out without another glance at his defeated opponent.

Kerrigan waited a minute or two and then drifted into the billiard-room, where Streatfield and the two girls were standing, cues in hand, in a group. Rubin was not in the room. There was an awkward drop in the conversation as he came in and then Streatfield said abruptly, "No, damn it, I'm going to," and came forward.

"Look here, Mr—"

"Kerrigan."

"Mr Kerrigan. Did you lose a lot to Ilford?"

"More than I could afford," replied the young man, wondering if he dared to venture on a sickly smile, and discarding it at the last moment in favour of a downcast expression. "About twenty-three pounds."

"It's a damned shame!" cried Rosemary Shackleford.

"He's a very good player," murmured Kerrigan deprecatingly.

"He's more than a good player," replied Streatfield meaningly. "He's a very lucky player. His luck is so famous that there are certain clubs in London where he finds it difficult to get opponents."

"I certainly thought he was a little fortunate once or twice this evening."

"Take my advice," replied Streatfield, "and don't play with him again."

"But I want to try and win my money back!" Kerrigan protested eagerly.

"When you've seen a twentieth part of the world that I have," said Streatfield, "you'll realise that you very seldom get your money back from men like him. Anyway"—he shrugged his shoulders"—don't say you haven't been warned."

"Thank you very much. Thank you very much indeed. But I assure you that I can look after myself. I'm not such a greenhorn as all that, you know. And now what about a game of bridge?"

But the other three declined, on account of the lateness of the hour, and retired. Kerrigan picked up a cue and began to practice some intricate fancy strokes at the top of the table, when the door opened and Mr Rubin came in. He stopped in the doorway for a moment, during which Kerrigan had the presence of mind to miscue atrociously, and then came forward.

"I'm glad to find you alone," said the American. "I've been wanting a word with you. Have a cigar?"

"No, thanks. I never smoke cigars," replied Kerrigan untruthfully. The other man lit up and then said: "Do you want to earn a little money, lad?"

"Absolutely." The reply was emphatic and sincere.

"Well, now's your chance. I don't know if you're a wealthy man or whether fifty pounds would be of any use to you. But if you want to pick up fifty, you can do it."

"Fifty pounds! I'm your man. It's nothing illegal, is it?" he added virtuously.

Mr Rubin laughed.

"Illegal! Good heavens, no. I want to send a letter to my wife about a business deal I'm engaged on, and the cops have established what you might call a censorship bureau here, and they're reading all the letters that come in or go out. Now, I don't want my affairs known to every Tom, Dick, and Harry in the Force. So will you slip out tonight and post a letter for me in Bicester?"

"Why not do it yourself?"

Mr Rubin looked at him pityingly.

"I was in the house when the librarian was bumped off," he said, "and so I'm a suspect. You weren't, so you aren't, if you follow me. We're under parole not to leave the house. I can't break my parole. Besides," he added naïvely, "it would look so damned suspicious if I was caught. But it wouldn't matter to you. You've given no parole and you're a free citizen. How about it?"

"I'll do it," said Kerrigan; "I'm a married man with seven children, and I couldn't look them in the face again if I refused a chance of picking up fifty pounds."

"Good lad, good lad!" exclaimed Mr Rubin. "I thought you'd probably help me. Here's the letter, and here's ten pounds to go on with. I wouldn't have bothered you, only it is very important. Vast sums of money are involved." He thrust an envelope and a crinkly note into Kerrigan's hand, and got up and hurried from the room.

"Well, now," murmured Kerrigan, lying back in his chair and gazing at the ceiling, "what on earth is the meaning of that? Am I behaving like such a complete mutt that people think I won't see anything fishy in being given fifty quid to post a letter at midnight? Or is Mr Rubin such a complete mutt as not to see anything fishy? Or is Mr Rubin a sufficiently clever man to see that I'm not such a fool as I look, and that I'll spot at once the fishiness of the transaction? Yes, that might be it. That might very well be it."

The letter was addressed to Mrs H. Rubin, 38 Edward Road, Battersea, and marked, "To be called for."

Kerrigan rang the bell and asked for a kettle of boiling water. With the aid of the electric heater he managed to maintain a sufficient head of steam to soften the gum of the envelope. Very gingerly he opened and read the letter. It ran:

"DEAR MARY,—You will find the stuff at 150 Ladbroke Crescent. But it is quite unimportant. Business is going fine, and I hope to complete soon. Please send me any news you get from New York.—

Yours ever,
            HILLDROP R. RUBIN."

He read it again and then a third time, and then he replaced it in the envelope and sealed it up. He was faced with a pretty problem, and the more he considered it, the more difficult it became. If it was a serious, urgent message, worth fifty pounds to get sent off, then it was obviously in cipher and might mean anything. No one in their senses would entrust an important message to a total stranger without making certain that it was unintelligible to him. On the other hand, it might mean nothing at all, in which case Mr Rubin must be trying to test the *bona fides* of the insurance agent. "That is to say," thought Kerrigan, "if I am a good man and true, I will go and post the letter and earn my money; whereas if I am a police spy, I will tell Fleming, and 38 Edward Street, Battersea, will be watched for little Mary, and 150 Ladbroke Crescent will be searched, and Hilldrop K.—Good Lord! what a name!—will know where I stand. But then again! Is he likely to pay fifty pounds to know where I stand? If so—he's up to no good, and that black-faced barrister isn't far wrong."

After half an hour's earnest pondering he left the billiard-room, nodded good-night to the sleepy policeman who was on duty in the hall, and strolled down one of the long ground-floor corridors as if going to his bedroom. It was now just on midnight, and the house was very quiet. On reaching the door of the gun-room in which he had found the plan of the house, he glanced over his shoulder to make certain that he was not being followed, slipped in and shut the door and wedged a chair under the handle. Then, very cautiously, without turning on the light, he tiptoed to a corner in which he had seen a jumble of tennis racquets and shoes, found a rubber-soled pair that more or less fitted him, opened the window noiselessly and peered out. A policeman was standing on the lawn about three yards away, with his back to him, yawning heavily. Peter Kerrigan ducked down below the level of the sill, and then slowly hoisted himself up so that he could just see over it and reconnoitred the position. The solution to the problem was easy. Twenty yards to the left a small conservatory was joined on to the house, and with a dexterous flick, Kerrigan threw a tennis racquet through the glass. The policeman gasped, drew his truncheon, and made a gallant sprint to the scene of the crash, while Kerrigan hopped out of the window, pulled it down after him, and scuttled along the shadow of the wall of the house, round a corner, behind a shrubbery, and down a garden walk in the direction of the wood which screened Marsh Manor from the road.

Once in the shelter of the wood he was comparatively safe until he reached the walls of the park, which were, for all he knew, also being patrolled by guardians of the King's Peace. He kept well away from the gates, and found himself confronted by the distinctly awkward obstacle of a twelve-foot brick wall, along the foot of which he groped in search of a foothold, until he suddenly came upon a ladder leaning against it. Without a moment's hesitation he went up it like a lamplighter, down the rope-ladder which was hanging on the other side, and off down the road in the direction of Bicester.

"I'm not the only cat upon the tiles tonight," he reflected, as he lolloped along at a steady six miles an hour into the town. He posted the letter, and then went into a day-and-night telephone box which was outside the post office and rang up the quiet little club at the back of Grosvenor Square that he belonged to—a club where a little roulette could always be played—and asked for the secretary. The secretary, whose real work did not begin until about one a.m. when the club-rooms began to fill up, was promptly available, and Kerrigan asked him to find out what he could about Sir George Ilford, Captain Streatfield, and Lord Claydon, and let him have the information sent to Jessop Gaukrodger, Esq., C.B.E., c/o The Angel Hotel, Bicester, to be left till called for. The secretary, whose terms for inquiring into antecedents were five pounds per head, willingly undertook the commission, and Peter, well satisfied with his evening's work so far, hung up the receiver, stepped out of the box, and collided with Miss Shackleford.

"Good evening, Mr Kerrigan," she said politely, and entered the box.

Peter Kerrigan walked very thoughtfully down the road for a couple of hundred yards and then, very thoughtfully, back again. The girl came out of the telephone box as he came up.

"May I have the honour of escorting you back to the Manor?" he asked.

"Of two evils, I would sooner be escorted than spied upon," she replied coldly.

"I wasn't spying upon you," protested Kerrigan.

"Let us call it simply a curious coincidence," answered Miss Shackleford, falling into step beside him. "And how is the insurance business? Flourishing, I hope?"

"Fair to middling, thank you."

"There are two rather queer things about you, Mr Kerrigan—by the way, am I walking too fast for you?"

"I can manage to keep up," he replied a little angrily. He made rather a speciality of self-possession and aplomb, but this girl seemed to be in the same line of business.

"You are much too well dressed to be an insurance agent, and much too foolish—after losing all that money to Sir George—to be anything except what you obviously are."

"And what is that, please?"

She laughed; a gay laugh which rippled away over the fields, and said:

"You're so obviously a society journalist. Tell me, are you Melisande, or Man About Town, or Cicerone?"

"As a matter of fact, I'm Lord Beaverbrook."

"Then will you give me a photograph and a couple of paragraphs in the *Express?*"

Peter Kerrigan changed the subject abruptly.

"Miss Shackleford, what is the trouble at Marsh Manor? There's no use telling me that there isn't any trouble, because it's so obvious."

"Do you suppose I would tell anything important to a gossip-writer?"

"Then there is something important?"

"Only to the people concerned. Not to you or your 'public.'" She threw an infinity of scorn into the last word. Kerrigan tried a new line.

"What sort of a man is Sir George Ilford?"

"Ask no questions and you'll get no lies."

"Oh! He's as bad as that, is he?"

"I didn't say so."

"And Captain Streatfield? He looks nice."

"He is nice."

"I suppose the truth is that Lord Claydon has made some sort of bloomer or other and Ilford is blackmailing him." Kerrigan spoke in jest, but he was immediately conscious that the girl's cheerful bantering defence had changed into a wary caution. There was a perceptible pause before she replied:

"That would make a good paragraph, wouldn't it? I expect you'd get seven-and-sixpence for that, and your boss would get a nice libel action."

"Ilford doesn't look as if he would stick at anything," Kerrigan reflected aloud. "Not the sort of man I'd care to come up against."

"Considering he was a heavy-weight boxing champion and is still in first-class condition, I don't advise you to come up against him, *mon cher petit.* What are you, five feet two, or five feet three?"

"Five feet ten," said Kerrigan indignantly.

"You don't look it," the girl replied with a maliciously bland smile. "I'm rather good at ju-jitsu and I believe I could take you on myself."

Kerrigan ignored this insult.

"What about the Treasure?" he asked, and this time she replied seriously:

"Ah! the Treasure. If only that could be found, it would solve everything."

"Are there so many things to be solved?"

"A good many," she sighed involuntarily.

"Such as?"

She recovered at once.

"Ah! That's asking. You stick to the Treasure hunt and the murder, and leave our private affairs to ourselves."

They trudged on in silence for a bit and then Kerrigan said:

"If I found the Treasure for you, it would be a help to you all, I understand?"

"If you found it after I've failed, it would be a miracle," retorted Miss Shackleford.

"Oh! So you've looked for it?"

"Everyone has looked for it."

"Except me."

She laughed derisively.

"Except, O most intelligent insurance agent, you!"

"Do you happen to know what it consists of?"

"Nobody knows for certain. But it oughtn't to be very hard to make a guess, when you remember that the mad Lord Claydon went in 1819 to stay with his friend the Maharajah of Futtiwalla; that while he was there he succeeded in persuading his cousin, the Governor-General, not to annex Futtiwalla; that the Maharajah was very grateful to him; that the Maharajah owned the finest collection of diamonds in India—which means the world—and that Lord Claydon came back from India with no more baggage than he took out."

"You mean you think the famous Treasure is a wad of diamonds?"

"I mean," she replied with mock gravity, "that I think the famous Treasure is a wad of diamonds. How exceptionally brilliant of you to guess my meaning like that!"

"It's my exceptional brilliance," murmured Kerrigan, "that has brought me to my present journalistic eminence. And now what about those ladders? They are yours, I presume?"

She nodded.

"Yes, I pinched them from the tool-shed."

They got over the wall and threaded their way through the park till they reached the garden, where the girl halted.

"This is where we part," she whispered.

"Mayn't I help you to get in?" he whispered back. She shook her head decisively.

"If it was a question of gate-crashing, I would trust myself to your expert guidance. But I don't fancy you're cut out for desperate enterprises. Good-night." She nodded and vanished swiftly behind a huge rhododendron.

Kerrigan waited breathlessly for the challenge of a policeman, but nothing happened to break the stillness of the night. After five minutes he concluded that by some means or other the girl had managed to get into the house unobserved, and he crept round towards the gun-room. The policeman was no longer visible, and five minutes later Kerrigan was safely in bed.

V

Inspector Fleming

Inspector Fleming was a quiet, cautious man. When he was sent to take charge of a case, the Superintendent at Headquarters and the Commissioners knew perfectly well that no mistakes of routine would be made, that no line of investigation would remain unexplored, and that no theory would remain untested. Progress would not be brilliant. The investigation would not proceed by spectacular leaps and bounds. But good, solid, persevering work would be put into it by the Scottish inspector and his group of subordinates. When, therefore, Lord Claydon had telephoned the news that his librarian had been murdered, and added that the Buckinghamshire police had no objection to the collaboration of a Headquarters detective, the assistant commissioner had no hesitation in dispatching Fleming to Marsh Manor. He arrived at half-past ten in the morning, and by half-past two he was telephoning his first report to his Superintendent. The main points of his report were:

1. That the librarian, Walter Newman, had been found dead in his pyjamas in the library, pistol in hand, battered about the head with the library poker.
2. That the windows of the library were fastened on the inside, and that the total absence of any traces or footmarks on the rain-sodden grass, gravel, or flower-beds made it almost certainly "an inside job."
3. That there was any amount of incentive for burgling the library owing to the supposed existence of the famous Treasure.
4. That there were several people in the house capable of striking the violent blow which killed the man.
5. That the antecedents of these people required careful investigation, as well as those of the librarian.
6. That a Peter Kerrigan had turned up for some reason or other, but definitely for no good purpose.
7. That he would report again next day.

"Nothing for it but to wait till tomorrow, Maitland," the Inspector said to his sergeant, as he hung up the receiver. "There are eight men, including the butler and the two footmen, who might have struck the blow, and the one who did it can't get far away even if he makes a bolt for it. Tomorrow we ought to get some answers to our questions. To my mind, it lies between Ilford and Rubin. I don't like the looks of either of them."

The sergeant, who was a silent man, nodded and said nothing.

"It all hinges, of course," went on Fleming, "on this so-called Treasure. If we knew what it consisted of, we should be a good bit farther on."

"Money's money all the world over," said Maitland gloomily.

"Yes, but it makes a lot of difference what form it's in. For instance, if this treasure really consisted of diamonds, we know where we are. Our pals in the diamond-gangs will be after them. But if it's some work of art, as it very well might be, according to what they tell me about the old lunatic, the diamond fellows won't touch it, and we shall have to look around in the high-class smuggling circles. It might be a picture, for instance."

"No one would kill a man for a picture."

"Not even if he knew he could smuggle it into America and get a quarter of a million for it?"

"Well, it might be," conceded Maitland.

"There's another question. Is the Treasure still here, if it ever was here, or did our friend with the poker get away with it last night?"

"Ah!" was the sergeant's contribution to the solving of this knotty point.

"If what Kerrigan says is true—"

"Ah!" said the sergeant again, knowingly.

"Exactly," replied Fleming. "I know it's a big 'if'; but, if it is true, that man John Hone, while working here in the library, tumbled to the secret and went away. Why did he go away? Either to get away with the Treasure or to get help to get away with it. If the former, why is the librarian murdered six weeks later? If the latter, the Treasure must be too big for one man to lift by himself. And in that case, what the devil can it possibly consist of? I understand from Lord Claydon that they've gone through the place with a pocket comb about once every six months for a hundred years."

"Quite," replied the sergeant.

"And there's another thing," pursued Fleming. "What the blazes is Kerrigan doing here? He doesn't waste his time, you know. If Kerrigan's about the place, you may be quite sure that money's about the place too."

"Yes."

"Well, there's nothing for it but to wait till tomorrow."

At midnight, Fleming was aroused by a policeman with the singular story that a tennis racquet had been thrown through a conservatory roof for no apparent purpose. A careful examination of the racquet and the scene of the incident cast no light upon the affair and the Inspector retired to bed once more.

Next morning the sergeant handed him a bunch of replies to some of the questions he had asked by telephone and telegram the day before.

The information contained in these consisted of the following:

1. That Walter Newman, the murdered man, was unknown in librarian circles; that his certificates of examinations passed, and degrees attained, were forgeries; that the two credentials of former employers in London were forgeries.
2. That Sir George Ilford was a man who lived very near the border-line between legal and illegal methods of self-support; that he had never actually stepped over the line so far as Scotland Yard knew.
3. That Captain Streatfield's name was unknown to the Yard.
4. That Mr Tollemache was a genuine art-valuer, and himself the owner of a fine collection.
5. That Lord Claydon was thought to be in low financial water.

While Fleming was considering these replies, Kerrigan strolled in and greeted the Inspector cheerfully. "I've got a bit of news for you, venerable sir," he said, seating himself on the edge of the table, and ignoring Sergeant Maitland's indignant frown. "Comrade Rubin is a queer fish."

"Is that your news?"

"That's my news. I fancy that Comrade Rubin is anxious to know whether I'm connected with the police or not."

"What makes you think that?"

"Oh, just an idea of mine, that's all. You see, he realises that I'm easily the most formidable person in the house. Did you say anything?" he asked, turning politely to Maitland who had snorted ostentatiously. "No? Then use your handkerchief and don't sniff. You see, Fleming, Rubin posted a letter last night—"

"What!" exclaimed Fleming, "Rubin posted a letter last night? How?"

"I haven't the faintest idea," replied Kerrigan blandly. "All I know is that he posted it, and I'm fairly certain he'll be expecting an answer by telephone today; just a message to say that his letter arrived safely without policemen attached to its delivery."

Fleming looked hard at the young man who looked back unabashed.

"Kerrigan," he said finally. "You went out last night and posted Rubin's letter, and you threw a tennis racquet through the conservatory to distract attention while you went out or came in."

Kerrigan protested.

"You haven't a shadow of right to make such an accusation. You haven't got a shred of evidence."

"I haven't got a shred of evidence, but I'm a tolerably good guesser."

Kerrigan laughed cheerfully.

"Let's leave it at that, shall we?"

"For the time being," replied the detective dryly; "and now let me give you a bit of news. The librarian was a fake."

"Forged references?"

"Yes."

"Then a whole lot of it is as plain as a pikestaff," cried Kerrigan energetically. "Hone discovered the secret and went off to find a buyer—"

"Leaving the Treasure behind him—" put in Fleming.

"Yes, and the news leaked out and Newman came down—"

"And a rival also came down—"

"And bumped off Newman. What clever little chaps we are, to be sure!"

"But Newman didn't know where the treasure was," said Fleming, "otherwise he wouldn't have stayed here six weeks."

"But did the murderer know?"

"He might have known. Hone might be working with him."

"Then why didn't Hone come down in person?"

"That's true," said Fleming thoughtfully. "Of course, the murderer might have got hold of Hone and made him tell him. Hone's been missing now for six weeks."

"Why not try to find him?"

Fleming looked at Peter with interest.

"What a brilliant suggestion," he said admiringly. "I would certainly act on it immediately if it wasn't for the fact that the idea occurred to me about twenty hours ago, and I acted on it then."

"All right, all right, all right!" protested the young man. "I was only trying to help."

A policeman came in with a slip of paper and laid it in front of the Inspector. The latter glanced at it, glanced at Peter, and then read out: "Telephone message for Mr Rubin: 'Mary received his letter quite safely.' Sent from call-box in Jermyn Street."

"Well, Master Kerrigan, it looks as if you guessed right too."

"It's by guessing right that I make my living," he replied.

"Give this to Mr Rubin," went on Fleming to his sergeant, "and ask Lord

Claydon to be kind enough to come and speak to me. Kerrigan, sit over there in that corner and listen, but don't butt in. Do you understand?"

"Yes."

Lord Claydon came into the room a moment or two later. There was still a worried look in his eyes and a distrait expression on his face, and his whole appearance was slightly untidy as if he had shaved, dressed, and brushed his hair with his mind on other things. His grey, drooping moustache which concealed much of his mouth, wanted trimming, and his hands were stained with nicotine. He sat down in an easy-chair and then nervously sat bolt upright on the edge of it.

"I've got one or two more questions that I must ask you, Lord Claydon," said Fleming. "The first is this: did you take up Newman's references?"

"Only the two in London. Not the Canadian ones."

"And the two replies were satisfactory?"

"They were most enthusiastic."

"The addresses from which they were written were empty houses."

"I don't quite understand."

"The man or men who wrote those replies had got access somehow or other to two empty houses—one in Belgrave Square and the other in Mount Street, Mayfair."

"Yes, I remember those were the vicinities I wrote to."

"And they simply burgled the two houses—got your letters out of them and answered them."

"So Newman's testimonials were forged?"

"Yes."

Lord Claydon sighed heavily. "I suppose he was after the Treasure. It's the curse of this house."

"There's another question, Lord Claydon. You must excuse its rather personal nature. Are you in financial difficulties?"

"Yes," replied Lord Claydon simply.

"So the discovery of the Treasure means a very great deal to you?"

"I don't believe it exists. I have long ago given up the idea that it exists."

"And Mr Tollemache is down here to value your pictures for the purpose of selling them?"

"Yes. I am going to dispose of almost all my Old Masters."

"Very well," said Fleming, "that is all I wanted to ask just at present."

"What do you make of him?" he asked, after Lord Claydon had gone out.

"To tell you the truth I'm not very much interested in him," replied Kerrigan. "It's another member of the family that I want to know more about."

"Which one?"

"I'll give you another tip, my lad," went on Kerrigan, ignoring the question. "There were two telephone calls put through from the call-box at Bicester last night about half-past twelve. One was of no importance—"

"To your club in Davis Street," interrupted Fleming.

Kerrigan stared.

"You old fox!" he exclaimed, "do you mean to say you've got on to those calls? What was the other one?"

"Ah! the other one," said Fleming thoughtfully. "The other one was interesting. It was a lady ringing up a friend in London and asking for a bunch of skeleton keys to be brought down here."

"A bunch of skeleton keys!" echoed Kerrigan. "What the devil for?"

"Perhaps to open something with?"

"Don't try to be funny," replied Peter warmly. "I am now going off to pursue my researches into the only member of this family that I find intriguing. By the way, is all that you've told me confidential?"

"Oh, dear me, no! You can tell anyone anything."

Kerrigan went out, murmuring to himself, "Now, what the blazes did the old fox mean by that, I wonder? I must be jolly careful."

He strolled through the house till he came to the billiard-room, where he found the two girls sitting in a corner darning silk stockings. Rosemary Shackleford looked up with a trace of animation and said briskly, "Good morning," but the other girl frowned and went on with her work.

Kerrigan sat down opposite them with the words: "Do you mind if I watch some of the world's work in progress?"

Rosemary smiled and replied:

"Have you got your paragraphs sent off to your paper yet?"

Lady Pamela looked up sharply and said:

"If anything appears in the Press about us that we can trace to you, I'm going to get you horsewhipped."

"Do you know," answered Kerrigan earnestly, "that you have raised a point of exceptional interest to a student of progress and evolution like myself? You want to get me horsewhipped, and I've no doubt it would give you a very great deal of satisfaction. But I wonder very much if there's such a thing as a horsewhip in the whole of this establishment?"

Lady Pamela half turned her back on him with an angry movement. He went on:

"Of course, you could get me hit over the head with a spanner, or even tickled to death with carburettor needles, but a horsewhipping—no. Not in this twentieth century age of mechanics. Tell me, Lady Pamela, where can I find out more about your fascinating ancestor who started all this trouble with his diamonds and his what-nots?"

"There is a biography of him in every room in the house, I should think," she answered coldly.

"And what would you say were his chief characteristics?"

"Why not read the book and see for yourself, Mr—er—Kerrigan. Shall we take a stroll in the garden, Rosemary?"

Lady Pamela got up and turned her back completely on Kerrigan. But Miss Shackleford unexpectedly declined.

"No, I'm feeling lazy. I'm going to stay here." Lady Pamela obviously was annoyed by this refusal, for she answered in a voice of ice, "Very well, dear, so will I."

"Somehow or other," murmured Kerrigan reflectively, "Lady Pamela manages to conceal her affection for me."

"It wouldn't break her heart if you left the house," said Lady Pamela.

"But Fleming won't let any of us go," protested Kerrigan.

A quiet voice came from the doorway of the billiard-room:

"Anyone may go who wants to. The investigation is closed."

Fleming could move very quietly when he wanted to. Kerrigan spun round.

"Your sleuthing over?" he cried. "You have made an arrest?"

"Not yet. But I know all I need to know."

"And you're withdrawing your men?"

"We are leaving almost at once. The rest of my inquiry will take place in London. Lady Pamela, perhaps you will inform the rest of the house-party that they are free to come or go as they please"; and with that Fleming quietly went out again.

Lady Pamela said sharply:

"Well, that settles the hash of our young gossip-writer. Out you go."

"Certainly," replied Kerrigan, "but I must have one moment's conversation with Miss Shackleford."

"Must?" said Lady Pamela, raising her eyebrows.

"Must," replied Peter undaunted.

"Come out into the garden, Mr Kerrigan," said Miss Shackleford unexpectedly, and she led the way out. The young man followed with alacrity, and when they were out of earshot of the house, he stopped and said, "I should like to help you."

She stared at him for a moment and then burst into a gay laugh.

"The young knight-errant, eh? Journalist turned Galahad? I think that's too sweet of you."

"Quite so," he replied imperturbably. "I've got the impression that you need help—as well as skeleton keys."

The smile faded abruptly from her face.

"You were fifty yards down the road when I was telephoning; you couldn't have heard me."

"I didn't."

"Have you told the inspector?"

"The Inspector told me."

She gave him a long, searching glance. "Why did he tell you?" she said at length. "Why are you in the confidence of the police, I wonder?"

"The point is that I think you're up against trouble and I should like to help you."

"The point is," she retorted, "that I don't think I want any help, thank you; and even if I did, I'm not at all sure that you would be a very competent helper."

"Give me a trial."

"Oh, dear me, no," she replied firmly. "Anyone who lets George Ilford rook him at picquet must be the biggest donkey in England. Good-bye, Mr Kerrigan," she held out her hand, "and give me a little write-up occasionally in your Society Chatterings."

There was nothing more to be said. Kerrigan watched her walk with athletic, springy step round the corner of the house, and then he went in to look for Fleming. He was told that the Inspector had already left for London by motor-car.

There was nothing for it but to pack his bag, being careful to put in it a copy of the *Life* of the eccentric Lord Claydon, and telephone to Bicester for a car to take him to the station. Neither Lord Claydon nor any of the house-party were visible.

Two hours later Kerrigan drove up to Grosvenor House in a taxi, changed into an unobtrusive suit of dark blue, put on a pair of rubber-soled shoes, equipped himself with electric torch, flask, sandwiches, various apparatus for picking locks, and an easily portable rope ladder and, hiring a fast car from a firm of motor engineers in Albemarle Street, drove himself back towards Bicester. It was Wall Street to a dime that some sort of game would be afoot at Marsh Manor that night.

VI

The Second Murder

Kerrigan reached a small village called Launton, a mile or two from Bicester, at about six o'clock in the evening, and, not wishing to arrive at the scene of action before dusk, he went into the "Black Bull," the only public-house in the place, and ordered some beer, and sat down in a corner of the parlour to study the biography of the old Lord Claydon who had started all the trouble. He was interested, not in the details of his life, but only in the details of his character. If the treasure had not already been found by the murderer of Newman, there was still a chance for an intelligent man to find the secret. And Kerrigan was firmly convinced that the best way to do that, indeed the only way to do it, was to study the peculiarities of the man who had hidden it. Hone had presumably succeeded in finding it, and Peter felt strongly that what one man could do could be done again by another man. After two hours of steady reading and intermittent beer-drinking, he called for a pencil and piece of paper and jotted down the main characteristics of the old gentleman so far as they emerged in the biography, as follows:

1. A very rich man who did not mind what he spent on works of Art.
2. A very shrewd judge of values. Almost every picture, statue, manuscript, gem, tapestry, and piece of stained glass which he bought had enormously appreciated in value during the last hundred years.
3. A great traveller.
4. A very peculiar sense of humour. For example, he had a large and most elaborate cottage built on the estate, and then used it as a kennel for a tiny Belgian dog which he had taken a fancy to; took enormous delight in practical jokes, especially hoaxes that hurt and annoyed people.
5. Author of several books on Art and pamphlets on Shakespeare.
6. Inventing a mythical Treasure might have appealed to him as a capital joke on posterity, but, on the other hand,
7. His passion for works of Art, and all beautiful things, was something he never joked about.

8. Took a great pleasure in setting puzzles and traps for people. He built a complicated maze in the park, brought Italian workmen over to make secret panels and doors and passages in the Manor, all of which were discovered in the course of the numerous searches for the Treasure, and enjoyed, like a child, pressing springs for doors or boxes to open, or mechanical toys to start functioning.
9. With the exception of the famous Treasure, was never known to conceal a work of Art however valuable it might be. He loved showing them off and letting them lie about the house.
10. Intensely despised all his children for being complete Philistines. He gave them every opportunity of travel and education, but none of them took the slightest interest in anything except hunting and shooting and fishing.

Kerrigan reread these jottings several times over. The problem to be solved was: where would a man of that character be likely to hide a jewel or a work of Art that was superlatively valuable? And, incidentally, what else except jewels could be so superlatively valuable to a man who had Titian and Rembrandt and Franz Hals and Benvenuto Cellini all over his house?

It was certainly a possibility that the whole thing was a grim hoax upon his Philistine children, and that he went happy to his grave in the knowledge that they, who had no use for beautiful things, should spend their lives in looking feverishly for a work of Art that had never existed. But if this view was correct, then what had John Hone discovered, and why had Walter Newman been murdered? The thing was certainly worth pursuing on those grounds alone, and at nine o'clock Kerrigan left the "Black Bull" at Launton to continue the pursuit. He dawdled quietly along the country lanes until he was within a mile of Marsh Manor, and then he drove the car into a field and parked it under the concealment of an English hedge in summer-time, and set out on foot for his objective. Although he walked with his usual confident elasticity of step, he did not feel at all easy in his mind about the night before him. There were too many incalculable factors for his liking, too many people who had a hand to play in the game. Peter Kerrigan could be rash and reckless when it was necessary, but he infinitely preferred to win a hand by skill and prudence than by wild bravado. He liked to go into an adventure with his eyes open, his plans laid, and, if possible, an avenue of retreat behind him. But tonight he was venturing into uncharted seas, and he would need to be even more wide awake than usual. One of the troubles about it, of course, was the palpably obvious trap which Fleming had laid. Fleming must have decided that the Treasure was still in the library, and had called off his men in order to induce the murderer to make another shot at finding it. Probably Fleming was hiding in the library at that very moment, pistol in hand and whistle in mouth. That part of the evening's work was more or less plain sailing. In normal circumstances the murderer would not be such an inconceivable ass as to fall into such a simple trap. He would wait weeks, even months, before making another attempt. What made the situation so complicated was that there were almost certainly several people who wanted a few hours alone in the library. The murderer, if Kerrigan's theory was correct, was not the only man who knew of the existence of the Treasure. There was John Hone, for one, and there were the members of the Claydon family circle; however sceptical it had become after a hundred years of fruitless search, the Claydon family must have had their hopes of ultimate gain raised suddenly and drastically by the murder. And it was possible, indeed probable, that the late Newman had confederates. The result of this would naturally be that none of the searchers could afford to run the risk of delay; it was better to run the risk of falling into Fleming's trap than of letting a rival steal a march. And in any case, what did the trap amount to? To enter a library, even with intent to commit a felony, was not proof of murder. On the other hand, Fleming was undoubtedly a wily old fox, and there was no knowing what he might or might not have up his sleeve. It was altogether a puzzling problem, and Kerrigan, as he hooked his portable rope ladder on to the wall of Marsh Manor, came to the conclusion that he had not the faintest idea of what was likely to happen. The only thing he felt confident about was that something or other was certain to happen.

He moved silently across the park until he came to the protecting belt of wood, and, selecting a spot on the inner edge of the wood from which he could command an excellent view of the library, at a distance of about thirty yards, he lay down in a conveniently soft cluster of ferns, and waited for events.

At about half-past ten he saw Lord Claydon come out, smoking a cigar, and stand apparently wrapped in thought on the gravel path. Then Sir George Ilford joined him, and they talked together for a few moments and then went in again, and Kerrigan heard the sound of bolts on the inside of the French window. A minute later the lights in the drawing-room went out. It was obviously the beginning of the retirement of the party, for it was not long before the lights in the billiard-room and then the lights on the staircase were extinguished one by one, until by half-past eleven there was not a single light visible from Kerrigan's hiding-place.

"That's jolly fishy," murmured that gentleman into the ferns. "Why is nobody reading in bed, and why this singular unanimity in favour of an early night?"

He smiled with gentle satisfaction. His theories seemed to be working out correctly. Every one in the house was going to bed early, because every one wanted to be first into the library. But each person would be certain to wait a short time—even if it was only a quarter of an hour—before beginning operations, in order to let the rest of the house settle down to its slumbers. Peter Kerrigan, therefore, rose to his feet and slipped noiselessly into the shadow of a long, rose-clad pergola and thence to the dark lee of the library itself. It took him only a moment or two to force up with a penknife the catch of one of the windows, hoist himself nimbly on to the window-sill, and lower himself silently into the library.

Once inside, he closed the window and crouched on the floor, listening, listening with every ounce of tense concentration that he was capable of mustering. For five long minutes he remained motionless. But there was no sound in the great, dark, vaulted library except his own soft breathing. At last he decided that it was safe to begin creeping towards the place he had selected in his mind for his observation post, and foot by foot he stole, on all fours, to the spiral staircase and up it into the narrow gallery. Once or twice the stairs creaked under his weight and each time he stopped dead and waited for something unpleasant, such as a shout, a light, or a pistol bullet, to happen. But nothing did happen, and at last he reached his objective. Then with infinite care he built up a rampart of heavy books in front of him and crouched down to wait. "Nothing like books for stopping pistol bullets," he reflected. And then he smiled broadly. It was one of the few occasions in his life when he had found some use for literature.

The air in the library was oppressively heavy and filled with the musty smell of old bindings; it felt as if it had not been changed since the library had been built by the mad old lord. It was laden with the dust of generations and seemed to intensify the sinister atmosphere which the murder of the librarian had created. It was just the atmosphere for a brutal and violent murder. The leaden stillness of it was frightening. It seemed to have enjoyed the murder and to be waiting for another. If Peter Kerrigan had been the sort of person who was affected by atmospheres, he would have been exceedingly uncomfortable, if not actually frightened. As it was, he settled himself down behind his rampart and gave himself up to the problem of whether to wear a grey topper at the Derby or a grey bowler. He had some time ago promised himself that when he was really in funds again he would stand himself one or the other, and the time had now come to carry out the promise. He was just deciding in favour of the topper when he suddenly realised with an abrupt and painful shock that there was someone in the library just below him. It was the sound of a chair being moved an inch or two on the parquet floor that warned him, and he leant forward and stared down into the darkness. Nothing was visible, but he thought he could just detect the occasional noise of breathing. It was not the presence of someone else in the library that gave Kerrigan such a shock. After all, it was exactly what he was waiting for. It was the silence of the other man's entry that made him think. He would need to be very expert in the art of moving in the dark to make so little noise, and the more expert he was, the more formidable an adversary he would be. But Kerrigan had not much time for reflection, for a less expert mover-in-the-dark was cautiously opening the door of the library, entering, and closing it behind him. Then there was a long pause, broken only by the sound of an occasional shuffle or crack which Kerrigan guessed to be the rather clumsy movements of the newcomer. The first man, immediately below him, was absolutely motionless—like a spider who has felt the impact of the unfortunate fly against the web. Kerrigan began to be rather sorry for the second man. He was so obviously an amateur and the other was so obviously a professional.

The heavy, musty atmosphere of the library seemed to become more than ever sinister, and the silence seemed to be made even more oppressively profound by the knowledge that men were lurking in the darkness below. Kerrigan suddenly decided to create a diversion. He took a book from the top of his rampart and threw it over the balustrade of the balcony. It fell with a resounding crash and was followed instantaneously by a gasp from the direction of the door. There was not a sound from below the balcony, and Kerrigan was immensely impressed with the nerve of the hidden watcher. The other man, of course, was simply a mass of nerves—a man who ought never to have undertaken an enterprise of this kind. He was probably armed to the teeth, too, and might start banging bullets off at any moment in any direction. That was the worst of amateurs. They had no sort of sense when it came to an emergency.

The emergency arrived almost at once. A thin beam of light suddenly sprang into existence from a point about six yards from where Kerrigan reckoned that the professional spider was sitting, flickered round the room, and came to rest upon the crouching figure of Mr Rubin near the door. Instantly Mr Rubin straightened himself with a hoarse cry, whipped out a pistol, and blazed off a fusillade at the light. The fourth shot hit the globe and the light went out. There was a moment of unearthly silence after the clatter. And then there was a gentle laugh from under the balcony, followed by a single shot and a heavy thud.

The whole thing had happened so swiftly that by comparison it seemed hours before the main lights of the library were switched on, and Fleming and three men in plain clothes came tearing up the library from the far end.

Actually it could not have been more than ten seconds. But the ten seconds had been enough. Mr Rubin lay dead on the floor with a pistol bullet through the heart, and an open window showed how the assassin had retreated. Fleming, pistol in hand, was out of the window in a flash and his men tumbled out after him.

The next moment there was a burst of sound as a powerful motor-bicycle engine sprang into life with a deafening roar.

VII

The Sampler Clue

There were obviously two men concerned in it, and they vanished into thin air, leaving few traces behind except evidence of remarkable audacity. So far as Fleming could reconstruct it, the sequence of events had been as follows: on the afternoon of the same day a powerful motor-bicycle and side-car had been stolen from the parking-place in the main square of Aylesbury. After dark, it had been driven to some spot fairly near the entrance of Marsh Manor, and then pushed by hand the rest of the way, through the gates, and up to a strategic position near the library. There were distinct traces of two different sets of footmarks beside the spot, where a small patch of oil showed that the machine had been parked. One man, whose feet left large imprints, had remained by the machine and chewed gum, while the other, obviously much smaller and lighter, entered the library. Only a second or two elapsed between the shooting of Rubin and the starting of the engine, and the same man could not possibly have managed both. In all probability the machine had started before the murderer reached it and threw himself into the side-car, so swiftly was the retreat effected. Indeed, the whole thing was so swiftly and efficiently carried out that Fleming never actually caught sight of either man. The outer cordon of police, guarding the walls and gates, had been withdrawn in order to encourage as many people as possible to walk into Fleming's trap, and, of course, one effect of this was to enable a fugitive who had once got clear of the house, to complete his escape with comparative ease in the darkness; and it was fair to presume that the raiders had known about the withdrawal of the cordon before they took the risk of entering the grounds of the Manor.

The motor-bicycle and side-car was found next day in a ditch near Banbury.

During the time which elapsed between the flight of the murderer and the return of the pursuing police-officers, Kerrigan hastily locked the door of the library and made a quick survey of the scene, ignoring the hammering and shouting which was soon in full cry on the other side of the door. Rubin was stone dead. That was obvious. He was still clutching his pistol in his hand, and the floor beside him was littered with empty cartridges. Below the balcony, where the single shot had been fired from, Kerrigan thought he could detect the marks in the dust where the man had knelt behind the desk. A large picture had been unhooked from the wall and was lying on the desk, but Kerrigan had no means of knowing whether the murderer had put it there or not. On the ground lay a contrivance which particularly interested him. It was a long flexible arm of steel, to one end of which was fixed the remains of the shattered electric torch, and which could be expanded to a length of about twenty-five feet or folded up till it was only a few inches long. It reminded Kerrigan of the arms for holding telephones which he had seen occasionally in offices, and the use of it was perfectly clear. He had, indeed, just seen a very convincing demonstration of its effectiveness.

At the far end of the library, he poked his head into the librarian's office where the detectives had been concealed, but there was nothing of interest there. He longed to search Rubin's pockets, but felt that that would be going a bit too far and that Fleming would make a real fuss about it "and I wouldn't blame him," he reflected with characteristic candour.

When the Inspector returned, he found Kerrigan seated at a table, smoking a cigarette.

"Oh, so you've come back?" he said shortly. Fleming was not in a good temper.

"Yes, and I'm full of information—"

He described briefly what he had seen, while the Inspector removed everything of interest from the dead man's pockets, and glanced through one or two letters and papers which he found in them. By the time he had finished, Fleming's natural good-humour had reasserted itself.

"The whole thing is my fault," he observed thoughtfully. "I completely underestimated the capabilities of the man; and yours, too, if it comes to that. I never thought for a moment that on a dead-calm night like this anyone could break in here without my hearing him from that end of the room; even though I did leave all the windows on the catch and oiled all the hinges. I didn't want to scare anyone away." He looked down at the dead body. "It would have been a good deal better for that poor fellow if I had scared him away."

"I suppose Rubin killed Newman?" asked Kerrigan. "Yes. I suspected him from the beginning, but I had no evidence against him. There isn't much against him now, except perhaps this." He held out a telegram which he had taken from Rubin's pocket, "And this wouldn't have hanged him."

Kerrigan looked at it and read, "W.N. is one of D.'s men." He nodded.

"I see. Someone warned him that Newman was a member of some other troupe of humourists; Rubin slugged Newman on the head, and another gent. comes down hot-foot to settle the account with Rubin. Perhaps it was D. himself. It's like one of those plays about Chicago that one reads about."

"Both Rubin and Newman came from America," replied Fleming significantly.

"So they did. And Ilford and Lord Claydon were both in America for a good many years:"

"Yes. And now, young Kerrigan, I've got to get to work. Run away home, and don't do any more burglarious entries into country houses. I ought to charge you as it is, but I'm not going to—I'm too busy. But you've got to promise to behave."

"It's no good," said Kerrigan, "I don't know how."

"Well, one of these days you'll run up against an officer who doesn't understand your temperament, and then you'll get into trouble:"

"And you'll bail me out, old chap. By the way, Fleming, was that picture on the wall or on the desk when you were here this afternoon?"

"I rather think on the wall. Incidentally, it isn't a picture. It's a sampler. Don't touch it, you young fool," he added sharply.

"You don't imagine," said Kerrigan, "that the man who moved about this room like a cat, who killed Rubin, and got away under your very nose—you don't imagine that he's left any finger-prints lying about?"

"You never know. And I'm not taking any risks."

"All right. I won't touch it. But what the blazes did he want with it? What is it, anyway?"

"It" was an old-fashioned sampler, consisting of lines of poetry exquisitely sewn in red and blue wool on a dark-grey background.

"Oh, I'll tell you what this is," said Kerrigan confidently. "It's the clue to the whereabouts of the diamonds. It's exactly what I'm looking for." Fleming smiled.

"It may be, or it may not be."

It all depends whether someone else unhooked it and laid it on the desk or whether our murderous friend did it. Dash it all, Fleming. I think you might have noticed whether it was on the desk this afternoon."

"I might as well point out to you, before I ask you to clear out, that it is one of a set of twenty-four samplers on the walls of this library; and that any of the other twenty-three are just as likely to contain the clue."

"Yes," murmured Kerrigan, eagerly scrutinising the sampler; "but the point is, why did the fellow unhook this one—or why did anyone else unhook this one?" He ran to where another of the set was hanging and peered at its edges, its frame, and glass, and finally unhooked it and examined the wall behind it.

"There you are!" he announced in triumph. "What did I tell you? This one is not only twice as dusty, but the mark on the wall behind it is twice as distinct; which means that it has hung here much longer, and that's because old John Hone had that one down when he was solving the key to the problem."

"You're an optimist," said Fleming, "and now—run away."

"I'm not going to leave this house until I've had a quiet half-hour with that sampler."

Fleming unlocked the door and held it open.

"You needn't leave the house, so far as I'm concerned. That's a matter for you and Lord Claydon. But you're going to leave this library."

There was nothing for it but to withdraw gracefully, and Kerrigan withdrew. He found the rest of the house in a turmoil of excitement. The house-party was assembled in the drawing-room, in varying types of dressing-gown, kimono, or overcoat, while the passages were full of the peering white faces and round eyes of startled domestics. Kerrigan marched boldly into the drawing-room, and there was a dead silence as he entered. Lord Claydon, curiosity completely overcoming astonishment and distaste, hurried forward to greet him with a flood of excited questions. What was it all about? Who had fired, and who at? Had anybody been hit? Was anyone hurt? What did it all mean? Where were the police?

Kerrigan advanced slowly, hastily revolving in his mind what he ought to say. By the time he had reached the middle of the room he had decided upon a policy which he thought would meet the case. He put on a lugubrious expression, shook his head sadly several times, and murmured, "An eye for an eye, a tooth for a tooth."

Lord Claydon stepped back in astonishment. "What do you mean?" he asked sharply.

Kerrigan shook his head again and said mournfully: "Mr Rubin killed Mr Newman, and now someone else has killed Mr Rubin. An eye for an eye."

Sir George Ilford, who had been standing by the fireplace, meditatively, with an arm on the mantelpiece, suddenly came forward.

"And who killed Rubin?" he demanded energetically. "You seem to be a little Mister Know-all. Can you tell me that?"

Kerrigan had intended to keep the conversation on a melancholy level. In the back of his mind he was toying with the idea of claiming that one or other of the dead men was his brother, in order to command sympathy and consideration, and, above all, an invitation to stay on in the house. But unfortunately his sense of humour ran away with him, and he could not resist the temptation to exclaim, with a hearty laugh, "Who killed Cock Rubin, eh?"

He regretted it the moment he had said it, because it raised the atmosphere from a suitable gloom into one of ill-suppressed relief. It was obvious that no one felt any profound regret for the demise of the American. Lord Claydon's tired and worried expression relaxed, and Rosemary Shackleford laughed aloud. Only Captain Streatfield was rather shocked.

"Oh, I say, Rosemary—come," he began, but the girl cut him short.

"Don't be a prude!" she exclaimed. "I'm sorry he's dead. I'm sorry for anyone that dies, but I'm not going to break my heart over a stranger whom I didn't very much like."

"I think you're perfectly right," said Kerrigan approvingly.

There seemed to be something in his voice, or perhaps in his very existence, that infuriated Ilford, for the huge baronet turned on him in a flash.

"You just shut up," he said fiercely. "No one wants your opinion, you damned little police-spy. The sooner you get out the better."

"I was going to suggest," replied Peter imperturbably, "that the longer I stay in, the better. In other words, as Mr Robey would say, that you invite me to join the house-party."

A moment of incredulous silence greeted this outrageous suggestion, and then Ilford said:

"Well, I'm damned!"

Lady Pamela merely remarked:

"You'd better ask Inspector Fleming if he has an official status, dad. If he has, he can go to the servants' hall—"

"And if he hasn't," Ilford chimed in, "he can go to hell!"

Kerrigan saw that the tide of public opinion was running against him. He determined on bold measures.

"Before you do anything rash," he said, holding up his hand as if he was a preacher exhorting his flock, "allow me to observe that I have no official or unofficial position—"

"Then it's outside for you, my lad," interrupted Ilford.

"But I do happen," went on Kerrigan, unmoved, "to be in possession of rather an interesting piece of information. It's about the famous Treasure." Lord Claydon turned sharply.

"It doesn't exist. There never was such a thing." The benign Mr Tollemache, who had been sitting unobtrusively in a corner of the room, got up at these words and came into the circle. He was wearing an old, untidy dressing-gown and a pair of grey woollen pyjamas and purple socks.

"I'm greatly interested in the Treasure," he announced in mild, precise tones, "as indeed every one naturally is."

"It doesn't exist," reiterated Lord Claydon. He was a man of one idea at a time. "If it had existed, it would have been found years ago."

Mr Tollemache looked inquiringly at Kerrigan. "Perhaps this young gentleman can give us some further enlightenment."

"I'm quite sure he can't," said Lord Claydon. Sir George Ilford added:

"If he takes my advice, he'll keep his mouth shut and clear out."

The two girls and Streatfield said nothing, but were watching keenly.

"But I don't want to clear out," protested Kerrigan. "If there's one person in the world who can help you to find this stuff, I'm that very same fellow."

Just as Lord Claydon was hesitating over his reply, Ilford said:

"Hang it all, Tom, we can't stay here all night. Give the man a bed, and sling him out in the morning."

"An admirable suggestion," said the adventurer. "Suits me down to the ground."

"That's lucky," replied Ilford grimly. "Come on." Without waiting for a word from the owner of the house or his daughter, Ilford marched to the door and led the way out into the corridor. Kerrigan followed him to a spare bedroom on the first floor and stood in silence while the other closed the shutters, bolted them, locked the small padlock on the bolt and pocketed the key.

"We don't want any more trouble tonight," he remarked significantly. "Sleep well," and he went out and locked the door behind him, leaving Kerrigan a prisoner.

About thirty seconds later Kerrigan had turned the lock of the door with a piece of bent wire, and was peering cautiously out into the corridor. He was just debating whether to venture out upon a general tour of reconnaissance when he heard the sound of shuffling and whispering upon the stairs and he hastily drew back and closed his door. A moment or two later, Streatfield and the two girls came in unceremoniously, almost pushing him out of the way as they did so, and Streatfield put his back against the door and pulled a heavy Service revolver out of his pocket.

"Now, Master Kerrigan, we want a few words with you," he remarked in a dry, menacing voice. Kerrigan stared at him, trying to estimate exactly how dangerous he might turn out to be. He was thin and square-shouldered and broad, and, although he was not much taller than Kerrigan himself, he looked strong and athletic. His face, the adventurer noticed for the first time, was tanned, not with the reddish hue of a few days in the English sun, but with the genuine, deep, permanent tan which is only produced by a long period in a tropical country. And people who spend long periods in tropical countries might easily turn out to have acquired rough ideas and efficient methods of putting their ideas into practice. On the other hand, he might simply turn out to be the ordinary type which goes from public school to the army or the Indian or Colonial Civil Service.

The two girls stood near the window—Lady Pamela looking at Streatfield,

Rosemary with her eyes fixed on Kerrigan. Streatfield proceeded at once:

"First of all, who are you?"

"A rolling stone," was the prompt reply.

"H'm! Gathering any moss that comes handy, eh?"

"Exactly."

"And at the moment you're after this Treasure?"

"My dear Sherlock, it's a treat to watch your giant brain at work."

"And you've discovered something?"

Kerrigan became cautious. He tapped the side of his nose with his forefinger and said, "Ah!"

"We want to know what it is," went on Streatfield, "and unless you tell us, there's going to be another shooting incident in this house."

"Dear me!" murmured Kerrigan absently, "how perfectly charming!" He was wondering what line of policy would be the most advantageous to himself. He held a good many cards, but on the other hand the trio which faced him held the supremely important card of entry into the library. He himself could hardly hope to go on entering the library an indefinite number of times by burglarious methods. And unless he did get in, his chances of being able to go on with the search were non-existent. He made up his mind quickly.

"Won't you sit down, ladies," he said, with his most charming smile. "I wish I had something to offer you to drink, but I fear it is hardly possible. It's not my house, you know," he added, with a bow to Lady Pamela.

"Well, come on," said Streatfield. "Out with it."

"I have a business proposal to make—" began Kerrigan, but the other cut him short.

"No, you haven't. We want to know what you know. That's all." He pointed the revolver at Kerrigan's chest.

"Hi!" exclaimed the latter in alarm. "Look out! That beastly thing is probably loaded."

"It is," was the dry answer.

"Well, don't point it at me. It's dangerous."

"It's only dangerous in the hands of people who don't know how to use it. I do."

"You ought to know, Mr Kerrigan," said Lady Pamela, "that we're in earnest. We don't care what happens so long as we get the diamonds."

Kerrigan faced her. "And why doesn't Lord Claydon want to find them?"

"Of course he wants to find them."

"I wonder. He seems so particularly insistent that there is no swag at all."

"I'm still waiting, Kerrigan," said Streatfield. "I'll give you three minutes.

After that—"

"After that, what?"

"I shall be compelled to send for my man-servant. He's waiting outside. He's a Colombian—you know—from South America. I may as well tell you that he is devoted to me, and that he's—er—inclined to be a little rough."

"No, Tom, I won't have it," cried Rosemary.

"You won't, but he will," was the quiet answer. Peter found himself more and more disliking the calm competence of this sunburnt captain.

"It's perfectly horrible," went on the girl, flushing up to her magnificent hair. "You're not savages."

"No, but my Colombian very nearly is," replied Streatfield, and Lady Pamela turned on Rosemary.

"We aren't doing this entirely for ourselves," she said.

"Who are you doing it for?" asked Kerrigan interestedly. "Your dog Fido?"

Lady Pamela looked at him with a cold, hard expression.

"You won't find the Colombian quite so funny!"

"But I say, have you appreciated the fact that the house is swarming with police?"

"You've probably had very little experience of a Colombian gag," murmured Streatfield, absently examining his revolver. "It's a singularly effective silencer.

"The whole story, please," said Lady Pamela, "beginning at the beginning. And please don't leave anything out or put anything in." Her voice sounded even more formidable than Streatfield's.

"How are you going to tell when I'm leaving things out or putting things in?" Kerrigan asked.

Streatfield replied slowly. "We know a good deal already, so you'd better be careful. Come on, now. Time's up."

Kerrigan looked at him and then at Lady Pamela, and then at Rosemary, and suddenly he felt sorry for them. They were so young and so earnest and so exceptionally foolish. Lady Pamela no longer looked formidable; she looked like a rather bad amateur actress. Rosemary ought to have been asleep in bed, dreaming of tennis-parties and dances, instead of being mixed up in childish melodrama. Streatfield, for all his grim expression and his sensational Colombian in the background, was a public schoolboy trying to impress his lady-love by a show of desperate valour and resource. Kerrigan smiled suddenly at them and sat down on the edge of the bed.

"Children, children!" he said, shaking a forefinger at them. "You're playing with fire. You're running yourselves into a deucedly complicated and dangerous business. And not one of the three of you is more than fifteen years old. Now don't interrupt, but listen to your wise old Uncle Peter. This, in fact, is the children's hour."

He then briefly sketched out the sequence of events which had led him from Mr Hone in the Euston Road to the spare bedroom in Marsh Manor, being very careful as he went along to omit any references to his skill at pocket-picking, at lock-turning, at window-opening, or any other accomplishment which might make him appear a man of knowledge and resource. They so obviously despised him that it would be a tactical error to disillusion them. He also forgot to mention that the man who shot Rubin had taken down the sampler from the wall of the library.

At the end of his story he said:

"That's all. And now I suggest that we join forces and hunt for this jolly old Treasure together." Streatfield opened his eyes ostentatiously wide at this suggestion.

"What an extraordinary idea!" he said. "We don't in the least want your help. We don't even want your company. If there's any money to be got, we're going to get it."

"Don't forget that the Claydon family has been after it for a hundred years," Kerrigan reminded him. "What makes you think you'll be more successful?"

"Never you mind," answered Streatfield. "Come on, Pamela. Come on, Rosemary."

"Then you won't combine with me?"

"Strange as it may seem, Mr What's-your-name, we won't."

Rosemary, who had been studying Kerrigan's face intently during his story, suddenly observed quietly: "Tom, do you realise that he hasn't said a word about his clue to the Treasure? Downstairs, he said that he had a clue."

"By Jove, you're right!" exclaimed Streatfield. "Come on, you blighter—out with it!"

"I'll show it to you tomorrow."

"You'll tell it to us now."

"But I'm getting very sleepy."

"At once, please!"

"All right, all right. Do put that pistol down! The clue I found was that the man who shot Mr Rubin was disturbed while looking at one of those samplers on the wall."

"Which one?"

"I couldn't describe which one, but I could point it out to you tomorrow."

"Come and point it out now."

"Don't be silly. The library is full of police." Streatfield seemed to see the force of this objection.

"All right. Tomorrow, as soon as we can get into the library, you'll show it to us. Don't forget. And, mind, no tricks—or—" He left the threat unfinished, opened the door and stood aside for the girls to go out.

"Au revoir, fair ladies," said Kerrigan. Lady Pamela walked out as if he did not exist, but Rosemary turned her head and looked at him curiously for a moment. She seemed to be puzzled by something about him. Streatfield, before going out, marched across the room and tested the padlock of the shutters.

"Have you got the key?" he demanded.

"No. The amiable bart. trousered it after telling me a bedtime story and kissing me good-night."

"Did he lock the door too?"

"He tried to," replied Kerrigan blandly, "but I don't think the lock works very well. Here is the key." Streatfield tested it. "Seems to work all right," he muttered and, going out, he locked the door and went off down the passage.

It was one of Peter Kerrigan's weaknesses that he could never resist the temptation to try to be funny. He would spend days laboriously building up a fictitious reputation and would then demolish it all in a moment by some idiotic and irresistible joke. The instant that Streatfield locked the door, the temptation surged up. In the twinkling of an eye he seized his bent wire again, unlocked the door, rolled a towel up into a ball, held it for a moment in the jug of cold water, and got into the corridor just in time to catch Streatfield on the back of the neck with a long shot as he turned the corner of the corridor. By the time Streatfield was hammering on the door, it was locked once again, and Kerrigan was vehemently protesting his innocence of the outrage.

His night's sleep was short, but it was very sweet.

VIII

Lady Caroline

At nine o'clock next morning the door of the bedroom was unlocked, and an extraordinary-looking man, who was obviously the Colombian man-servant, came in, carrying a breakfast-tray. He was very short and square, so square as to be almost deformed, and he was bow-legged. His arms were long and powerful and his depth of chest was remarkable. Black hair, close cropped, heavy black eyebrows, and a dark skin completed a singularly repulsive picture. Kerrigan blinked, and then sat up in bed and rubbed his eyes.

"Hullo, Tarzan," he observed at length, "so you've weighed in with the morning coco-nuts, eh? And how are things in the jungle?"

The man answered with a flood of Spanish and scowled. Kerrigan, who wasn't going to give away the fact that he once spent a hectic year in Venezuela and spoke Spanish perfectly, lay back and murmured genially, "Well, you are an ugly swob and no mistake."

The Colombian knew enough English to understand this, and to reply, "You laugh other side of your face soon!"

"Leave me, laddie, leave me," said Peter, waving to the door. "The sight of you is bad for the appetite. And, by the way, be a good little Señor and borrow me a razor."

"I shave you myself," suggested the man unexpectedly.

"You do nothing of the kind!" Kerrigan retorted with emphasis.

An hour later the young man once again picked the lock of his bedroom door, and strolled downstairs. Streatfield met him in the hall and stared. Kerrigan patted him on the shoulder in a kindly way.

"It was a faulty lock, old chap. I told you it was. I hope you slept well."

He strolled past him into the drawing-room and found Pamela talking to a new addition to the party: a venerable and rather severe-looking old lady, dressed in rustling black, and hung about with jet ornaments. Lord Claydon was standing uncomfortably in the background. Pamela started and frowned at the young man's entrance.

Streatfield, who had followed him, called out over his shoulder, "He's got out, somehow. But it's all right. I'll take care of him." He added in a venomous undertone and with an apprehensive glance at the old lady, "You come right out of here."

Kerrigan smiled, went forward, and bowed to Lady Pamela.

"I trust you had a quiet and pleasant night."

"Who is this, who is this?" exclaimed the old lady, fumbling for her lorgnette.

"It isn't anyone, Aunt Caroline, it's just a—just a—

"Insurance agent," said Streatfield, from behind. "You mustn't listen to old Tom Streatfield," said Kerrigan with an easy laugh. "That's his idea of a joke."

The old lady found and adjusted her glasses, examined the young man through them, and said to Pamela at the same time:

"Well, child, where are your manners, where are your manners? Introduce him to me."

"He isn't the sort of person that one introduces," replied Lady Pamela coldly.

The venerable lady turned upon her.

"I didn't ask you what sort of a person he is," she said in a voice that made Pamela's sound almost cordial. "I told you to introduce him."

The girl's pretty face grew dark and sulky as she muttered:

"Mr Costigan—my aunt—Lady Caroline Marsh."

"Kerrigan, not Costigan," he corrected cheerfully.

"Is your hair artificially waved, or is it naturally wavy, young man?" demanded the dame.

"It's the same as yours, madam—naturally wavy."

Lady Caroline was somewhat taken aback by this reply, and renewed her scrutiny with her glasses.

"I gather from the singularly unpleasant look upon my niece's face," resumed the old lady, "that you are not exactly *persona grata* here. Why is that? Are you a tradesman, or merely a poor man. You have the appearance of being a gentleman."

"That is one of the first things they teach us nowadays at Borstal," replied Kerrigan.

"Why don't they like you?" persisted Lady Caroline.

Streatfield started to say something about a misapprehension, and was sternly informed that his opinion would be welcome when asked for, but not a moment sooner.

"I can't make it out," replied Kerrigan. "I'm far and away the most amusing person in the house. I'm brimful with anecdotes about leading personages in all the capitals of Europe—"

"Scandalous anecdotes?" interrupted the old lady.

"Highly scandalous, madam. Not fit for your ears, I can assure you."

"Harry!" she cried, wheeling imperiously upon Lord Claydon, "I insist upon Mr Cartwright—"

"Kerrigan."

"Taking me in to dinner tonight."

"But, my dear Caroline," replied Lord Claydon, "you don't understand the circumstances. Mr Kerrigan isn't even staying in the house. I don't know anything about him."

"Pooh! Stuff and nonsense. I understand this, that two men have been murdered in this house within forty-eight hours of each other, that you are trying to sell the family pictures—which is a downright, damnable scandal—and that I've got to spend the next day or two here finding out what's at the bottom of it all, and that I insist upon Mr Kerosene—"

"Kerrigan."

". . . being invited to stay and entertain me. Otherwise I shall be bored to death by these thickheaded children, and glowered at by that intolerable George Ilford."

"I shall be delighted if Mr Kerrigan would stay," said his lordship gloomily.

"It's quite out of the question," said Pamela.

"Impossible." Streatfield shook his head emphatically.

"I accept your invitation with the greatest pleasure," remarked Kerrigan.

"Capital!" exclaimed the old lady vigorously. "Then that's settled. And now sit down here, Mr Kerrigan—got it at last!—and talk to me. Tell me about some of these capitals of Europe. Were you ever in Petersburg?"

"I was at school at Petersburg Academy. I was sacked after one term."

"Oh no, no, no! Come, come!" expostulated Lady Caroline. "You can't expect me to believe that!"

"It's quite true. It was in 1911."

"I was there nearly fifty years ago. My husband was ambassador. It was a lovely city. Ah! what times we had!"

"You must have been the toast of the town," said Kerrigan with a courtly bow. The old lady rapped him on the hand with her lorgnette and almost giggled. Lady Pamela walked out of the room indignantly, with Streatfield at her heels.

"Impertinent baggage!" exclaimed Lady Caroline. "You ought to spank her, Harry."

"Yes, quite so, quite so," murmured Lord Claydon, and he also went out.

The old lady's demeanour changed abruptly. She leant forward and whispered:

"What's up here? The whole place is at sixes and sevens."

"I can't make it out," Kerrigan whispered back. "But I know this, it's more than the murders. There's something else."

"Why should Harry be selling the pictures?" Lady Caroline hissed at him. "He was left three-quarters of a million, and he's lived quietly. And what is Ilford doing here?"

"I don't know anything about him."

"He's a bad lot, but he's as thick as thieves with Harry. Always has been."

"Perhaps the money for the pictures is going to Ilford?"

"Can't be that. If Ilford wanted money to get him out of one of his scrapes, Harry would give it to him in cash. He's got plenty."

Lady Caroline leant back and gazed at the ceiling for a moment. Then she fixed the young man with a hawk-like glance and said:

"And where do you come in? Police?"

"No. I'm on my own."

She looked at him again and then snapped:

"Rosemary?"

He shook his head. There was another pause, followed by:

"Adventurer, eh?"

Peter Kerrigan was a little startled by the old dame's shrewdness, especially as she followed up the thrust with another.

"After the Claydon Treasure, I suppose. Do you think you'll get it?"

"If it exists."

"How?"

"By using my brains."

She scrutinised him very carefully once again and said:

"You're frank, anyway. Well, your only chance of finding it is to stay in the house."

"Lady Caroline, you are a confoundedly sharp old party," said Kerrigan, and the old lady screamed with delighted laughter.

"And everyone else wants to chuck you out, and that's why they're so furious at my asking you to stay, and that's why you jumped at my invitation with such alacrity."

"Your ladyship goes right up to the top of the class!"

"Very well, Master Kerrigan. You're at my mercy. I'll make a bargain with you. Find the Treasure for me, and I'll give you one-tenth of it, for yourself."

Peter threw up his hands indignantly. "One-tenth! Oh, most generous lady!"

"Very well. I'll make it a fifth."

"I would suggest half and half."

"Oh, you would, would you!" replied Lady Caroline with spirit. "A fifth, or nothing. Don't you see, my man, that without me you're useless? You'd go out of the front door this minute. But I'm not quite useless without you. I've got some brains of my own."

"Let's make it a quarter," said Kerrigan, seeing immediately the force of her argument.

"You're a greedy young hound; very well, we'll make it a quarter. And mind you play fair or else—"

"I'll play fair," he assured her, but her shrewd old eyes twinkled with scepticism.

"I think you will while I'm watching you. But I wouldn't trust you an inch out of my sight. What's the next move, young man?"

"There is nothing to be done until the police leave the library. I don't know if the Treasure is there. But I am certain that the clue to its whereabouts is there. By the way, Lady Caroline, what do you think of Captain Tom Streatfield? Is he on the level? I mean, is he straight, or is he—"

"Another old Borstalian, eh?" Lady Caroline finished the sentence for him with a flicker of an ancient eyelid that was suspiciously like a wink. "I don't know anything about him," she went on. "He's engaged to Pamela, and so far as I'm concerned, he's welcome to her. She's a spoilt brat."

"We must keep an eye on him," said Peter. "He's after the Treasure, too, and he's got a man-servant that has dropped straight out of the primeval jungle."

The door opened and Mr Tollemache mooned benevolently into the room and bowed to Lady Caroline, who replied with a grim nod.

"A terrible, terrible business," the art-valuer said, wringing his hands nervously. "A second murder in such a short space of time. And such a nice man, such a very nice man. Why, only last night I was inviting him to come and see my small collection of Old Masters in London. Poor man! Poor, poor man!"

"Talking of Old Masters," said Lady Caroline with asperity—"who is going to buy my brother's collection?"

"I have found a buyer. I have my own humble little way of finding buyers, but sometimes they are successful. And in this case I am happy to say, I have found one who is willing to pay a good price for the chief pictures."

"What do you call a good price?"

"Alas! I am not at liberty to say. It is a matter of professional etiquette, you understand. Lady Caroline, may I have a word with you? If possible, alone?"

"Don't mind Mr Kerrigan. He's my secretary. Go on."

"Well, it is great intrusiveness on my part, meddling in a strictly family affair. But it did occur to me that a solution of Lord Claydon's financial troubles is to be found in the famous Claydon Treasure."

"First find the Treasure," put in the old lady dryly. "Oh, exactly, exactly." Mr Tollemache was very shy and nervous. "But what I was about to suggest is that we should all pool our brains and our ideas and help Lord Claydon to find it. I would be only too glad to do anything I can to assist."

"And what use would you be?" inquired Lady Caroline with brutal directness.

Mr Tollemache was flustered.

"I—er—thought that the Treasure might be a picture or a diamond or something that I'm accustomed to handling," he murmured disjointedly.

"Very well," replied Lady Caroline briskly, "if we want your help we'll let you know. Many thanks. Many thanks. And now, Mr Kerrigan, give me your arm. I'm going to sit in the summer-house." They went out, leaving the art-valuer behind them.

"Now what did he want?" asked the old lady, as soon as they were out of earshot.

"I'm not very sure," said Kerrigan slowly, "I haven't paid much attention to Comrade Tollemache up to now. Apparently he's a well-known art-collector and what not. Inspector Fleming verified his *bona fides*."

"His *bona fides* as an art-collector," said Lady Caroline sharply, "is one thing. His methods of collecting might be another. For all we know he may be a picture-thief."

"But not a murderer," protested Kerrigan. "Surely that grey-haired old dodderer doesn't sneak about at nights with guns and stuffed eel-skins!"

"I don't know what a stuffed eel-skin is, and I don't think I want to know. Now, wrap that rug round my feet, and hand me that book and go away. Come back the moment it is possible to get into the library."

Peter Kerrigan settled his new patroness into a long chair and went off in search of Inspector Fleming, reflecting as he went that the bargain he had made with Lady Caroline was probably the best thing he could have done in the circumstances. It was exasperating to have to promise to take only one quarter of the loot, but the philosophical way of regarding it was to remember that he was lucky to be inside Marsh Manor at all.

He found Fleming once more packing up to leave. "A genuine departure this time," the Inspector said with a grin. "I've no doubt whatever that Rubin killed Newman, and that the man who killed Rubin has got away from here. So I've got to get away from here too."

"What about the Colombian nightmare?" asked Kerrigan casually. "You don't think he had a hand in any of it?"

"Maybe aye and maybe no," was the non-committal answer. "In any case I know where to lay my hands on him when I want him."

"So you're really off?"

"I'm really off. You'll be wanted at the inquest, of course. I'll see you there. By the way, when you explain to the Coroner how you broke in last night, you may find the local cops slipping after you with warrants. So you'd better look out. I should be sorry to see you get thirty days; when you ultimately fetch up in jail, it ought to be for fifteen years at least."

As soon as Fleming and his assistants had departed, Kerrigan ran to the summer-house, awoke Lady Caroline, and conducted her to the library. The door was locked on the inside, and there was the sound of voices from within.

"Who's in there?" screamed the old lady through the keyhole. "Open the door this very instant."

The voices immediately stopped and there was silence inside. Lady Caroline repeated her shrill and vehement demands, beating upon the panels with a stick as she did so. Finally Pamela's cold, hard voice came from within.

"I'm very sorry, Aunt Caroline, but we're busy."

Streatfield's voice added, "Kerrigan, don't waste time picking the lock. There's a good stout bolt on this side of the door!"

"Come round and break a window," urged the old lady in a whisper. But her voice was more penetrating than she intended, for Streatfield replied at once:

"I'm afraid we've got them all shuttered, Lady Caroline. We're going to be here for some time."

The fiery blood of a hundred earls started into the wrinkled face of her venerable ladyship and her eyes sparkled with indignant fires. She was just about to launch more screams through the keyhole, when her new secretary held up a restraining finger and beckoned her back along the passage.

"Well, what is it?" she demanded. "If you've got an idea in your head, let's have it. Come on, man, come on."

"If they've got all the shutters up," whispered Kerrigan, "all we've got to do is to find the main electric-light switch and turn it off. They'll hate treasure-hunting in the dark."

Lady Caroline's fury gave way to a cackle of delighted laughter which echoed down the corridor. "Mr Crawshawe—"

"Kerrigan."

"Look here, young man," she exclaimed peremptorily, "I will not be interrupted and corrected by a whipper-snapper like you all the time. What's your Christian name?"

"Peter."

"Very well, Peter, you're an unmannerly lout to keep on interrupting an old woman, but that's a good idea of yours about the switch."

"I'll go and turn it off." The lapel of his coat was grasped by a small, plump, ring-bedecked hand. "Stay here, you young donkey. I'll turn the switch off. You must wait to see what they do. They'll either open the door or a shutter," and with that she marched off down the corridor, chuckling with elderly glee as she went.

Two or three minutes later a chorus of "Oh's!" from the library indicated that she had not taken very long to carry out her part in the manœuvre.

Then there was a long pause. Kerrigan, kneeling with his ear and eye alternately to the keyhole, could hear the muttered sounds of a council of war, and he was suffering from pins-and-needles and incipient cramp before he saw a thin ray of light from the direction of the windows, and knew that a shutter had been opened. He ran out into the garden, found the window that had been unbarred, flattened his nose against the glass, and started when he saw the ugly face of the half-deformed Colombian glaring at him from a distance of about two inches. The man was holding an unpleasant-looking knife in his right hand. Kerrigan stooped, heaved up a large stone from a rockery which happened to be at his feet, and discharged it accurately through the window-pane into the Colombian's face. The latter fell back with a howl of rage, and Kerrigan poked his head carefully through the hole in the glass and said:

"What cheer, chaps? Have you found the boodle?" The Colombian, with blood streaming down his face and a flood of Spanish oaths streaming from his lips, stood waving his knife like a maniac and was only calmed by a curt order in Spanish from his master, who came up to the window and said quietly to Peter:

"You're not doing yourself any good by these antics, you know. You'd very much better go away before anything serious happens to you. It's been a nasty house for accidents lately."

Streatfield looked very cool and very self-confident as he spoke, and again Peter had the feeling that he and his weird man-servant, though not conspicuously endowed with brains, would be a very awkward pair to meet in a rough-and-tumble on a dark night in an out-of-the-way spot. Rosemary Shackleford looked over his shoulder, and asked:

"Which of the samplers was it, Mr Kerrigan?"

"Let me in and I'll show you."

"Not blooming likely!" she replied gracefully.

"Then I'm afraid you'll just have to guess."

This conversation was interrupted by the appearance on the lawn of Sir George Ilford and Lord Claydon. During the brief exchanges which followed it was the dark baronet who did all the talking, while Lord Claydon stared at the ground and kicked at stray fir-cones.

"What's up?" demanded Ilford. "Lady Caroline says that there's some sort of shindy going on."

Kerrigan withdrew his head from the jagged hole in the glass and replied:

"It's only the Treasure-hunt, old chap. Streatfield's digging away like mad in the library, and Tarzan's on duty at the window. The glass broke," he added, "when Tarzan went too close to it."

"Damnation!" exclaimed Ilford, and he thrust his head through the hole and shouted, "Streatfield, you damnable fool! Who the devil asked you to butt in here?"

Streatfield answered coolly:

"And who the devil asked *you* to butt in here?"

"Lord Claydon did, and he happens to be the owner of this house. There isn't a Claydon Treasure, and even if there was, he wouldn't want you to look for it. Do you understand that?"

"Pamela wants me to find it, and I'm going to. Do you understand that?"

"Your turn, Sir George!" said Kerrigan, but the other did not hear him.

"Well, just listen to this," he was saying. "You clear out of this library, and don't worry Lord Claydon any more. He's got quite enough to worry him without all this." Ilford's great dark head came out of the hole and he addressed Kerrigan.

"And the same thing applies to you as well."

"And to me as well?" said a mild voice behind them, and they all wheeled round to find that little Mr Tollemache had unobtrusively joined the party. Lord Claydon turned away from him and walked across the lawn, as if the reminder of the impending sale of his art-treasures was more than he could stand.

"Yes, you as well," replied Ilford moodily.

"My own impression," said the little art-collector sunnily, "is that the famous Treasure is a picture or set of pictures of magnificence surpassing any that exist today—a collection, for instance, of Michaelangelo's lost cartoons, or unknown portraits by Velasquez, or pictures of Vermeer of Delft. Even if I am wrong in holding this view, surely the bare possibility that I might be right is enough to justify every man and woman in prosecuting this search to the very utmost of their ability. It is a duty which is owed to mankind, in the sacred name of Art."

"In the sacred name of drivel and balderdash," replied Ilford furiously. The timid Mr Tollemache shrank away from the big man's menacing tone and murmured something apologetic about being extremely sorry if he had said anything which upset anyone. Ilford swung round with an impatient snarl, and strode after the receding figure of Lord Claydon, leaving Mr Tollemache to appeal to Kerrigan against the injustice of the way in which his innocent remarks had been taken up. The latter looked at him thoughtfully.

"Yes, it certainly was odd," he said slowly; "very odd indeed."

He turned to see what the party in the library was doing, and saw that the door was standing wide open and the library was empty. They had taken advantage of the diversion created by Mr Tollemache to beat a retreat. Kerrigan raced round the house and dashed into the library. All the samplers had been taken off the walls and a heap of empty frames lay on one of the tables. A fanfare of an electric horn made him look up just in time to see Streatfield and the two girls, and the Colombian man-servant, tearing down the avenue in a huge, pale-blue Bentley.

IX

The Missing Book

Kerrigan was still watching the gap in the trees through which the Bentley had vanished several seconds before, when Lady Caroline tapped him on the shoulder.

"Well, so they've gone," she said. "Why?"

"It's all my fault," replied Kerrigan.

"I didn't ask whose fault it was. I asked why they've gone."

"Because they've got the samplers, and I suppose they've taken them away to some place where they can examine them at leisure."

"The samplers?"

"Yes. The man who murdered Rubin last night was examining one of them when he was interrupted. I told that bright young party that one of the twenty-four held the clue, but I didn't tell them which of the twenty-four it was; and in any case, I never dreamt that they would get in ahead of me. I completely underestimated Streatfield's resourcefulness."

"Streatfield's resourcefulness?" said the old woman scornfully. "The brains of the party is in that red-haired girl's head. She's as artful as a sack of weasels."

"The point is, what are we to do next?" replied Kerrigan, thinking very hard. "There are very odd things about this whole business. Why is Lord Claydon so very anxious that the Treasure should not be discovered? If he's as hard up as he appears to be—"

"He's not hard up at all," snapped Lady Caroline.

"But he's selling the pictures!"

"It's my opinion that the man's mad."

"It might be that he really has lost a very great deal of money and that he's already found and sold the family Treasure. That would account for his not wanting us or Streatfield to go on looking for it."

"Stop these idle speculations, young man, and tell me which of the samplers contains the clue."

"I couldn't tell you which one it was, Lady Caroline. I could only show you where it hung in the library, and that isn't much good."

"Come and show me," ordered Lady Caroline, and they went into the ill-omened room. Kerrigan pointed out the place where the sampler had hung. Lady Caroline pursed up her thin dry lips and looked with bright, bird-like glances up and down the walls, counting aloud, "one, two," up to six—over and over again. Finally she said, "I can whittle it down to one out of six. Those samplers were put up by the mad Lord Claydon about the same time as he built this library, and they were in sets of six, four sets of six each. One set was quotations from *Hamlet*, one from *Macbeth*, one from *Lear*, and one from *Othello*. This must have been one of the *Hamlet* set. I remember they started at that window there."

"When you say *Hamlet* and all the rest of it," said Kerrigan diffidently, "do you mean the stuff that Shakespeare wrote?"

Lady Caroline fumbled for her lorgnette and gazed at him with the utmost astonishment.

"Yes, I do mean the stuff that Shakespeare wrote."

"I thought you probably did. I'm not much of a reader myself. It's generally thought to be pretty high-class, isn't it?"

"It *is* generally thought to be pretty high-class," conceded Lady Caroline grimly.

"Dear, dear, dear!" said the mild voice of Mr Tollemache behind them. "What a scene of destruction and desolation! Who on earth has been cutting those charming Georgian samplers out of their frames? What Philistine has done this thing? If it was poor Mr Rubin, I can almost sympathise with the man who shot him, though I fear—ahem!—that that is rather an irreverent thing to say. *De mortuis nil nisi bonum*, so to speak."

Lady Caroline, whose lorgnettes were now in full blast, turned them upon him with cold dignity. "Quite so," she observed, and turned again to her new secretary.

But Mr Tollemache was undaunted by the obviousness of the snub. He was already examining the heap of frames with the close, peering scrutiny of the connoisseur.

"Fine old Georgian frames," he murmured, "but sadly pock-marked a long time ago by some scoundrel with a bodkin or some such instrument." He picked up one of them and swung it backwards and forwards. "Heavy things; no wonder the thief preferred to cut out the samplers and leave the frames."

"Were the samplers valuable?" asked Kerrigan sharply.

Mr Tollemache smiled a benignant smile.

"I would have offered a hundred pounds for the lot, if Lord Claydon had wanted to dispose of them. But perhaps a hundred guineas would have been nearer the mark. I am not sure," and the old man drifted out again aimlessly.

Kerrigan waited till he had gone and then said:

"If the value is not in the samplers as samplers, nor in the pock-marked frames—by the way, I wonder why the bodkin-holes in them? Oh yes, of course; some earlier generation of treasure-hunters—it must be something hidden between a sampler and the frame—"

"Of course not!" interrupted Lady Caroline indignantly. "Don't be so silly. If it had been that, why do you suppose they would have taken away all the samplers? And besides, it would have been found ages ago!"

"I beg your pardon, I beg your pardon, Lady C. Of course, you're right."

"Thank you. Of course I am."

"So the quotations must contain the clue. That's the only alternative left. And that blighter Streatfield has the quotations. Well, the only thing to do is to get after him. That blue Bentley is a fairly conspicuous car; it ought to be easy enough to follow."

"Would it not be as well to inquire," suggested Lady Caroline with a meekness that contrasted most suspiciously with her usual aggressive briskness, "whether copies of the samplers exist?"

Peter Kerrigan looked sharply at her and then observed with a laugh:

"Come on, now, Lady Machiavelli, out with it. Where are the copies?"

"How dare you address me so impertinently? Do you hear? As a matter of fact," she went on with another of her elderly chuckles, "there used to be drawings of them in a large album somewhere. Harry will know where it is."

"Will you ask him where it is, Lady Mac? It would come better from you than from me."

"Lady Mac? What new impertinence is this? Oh, I see! You young ruffian. Very well, I'll go and ask him. You wait here. I suppose that even you can see the significance of the existence of a book of copies of a lot of old samplers that aren't worth more than a hundred guineas today, and couldn't have been worth more than a hundred pence then." She shuffled out briskly, and Kerrigan could hear her chuckle as she went and exclaim, "Lady Mac indeed! I'll Lady Mac him!"

Sir George Ilford must have been waiting for an opportunity to speak to Kerrigan, for the moment the old lady had gone he appeared with all the well-timed promptness of a stage entry. He seemed to be in a great hurry and his long strides were even longer than usual.

"Look here, Kerrigan," he began at once, "this is all very unfortunate for Claydon. He's asked me to talk to you about it. Strict confidence and all that. Understand?"

"I shall have to use my own discretion about that," said Peter. "I'm not going to promise anything." Ilford considered this reply for a moment and then said:

"Very well, damn it, it can't be helped. Look here, it's about this infernal treasure-hunting of yours and old Lady C. and that triple-dyed fool Streatfield. One of you will go and find it, and that will be the ruin of Claydon."

"Why?"

"Because he's been doing some damned silly speculating and has got himself into an almighty hole and owes a packet. I can tell you, he absolutely owes a packet. The result is that all his pictures have got to go. But I've worked out an arrangement with his creditors by which they'll take part of the debt in cash, part of it in pictures, and let the rest go hang. In other words, they don't want to bankrupt Claydon and smash him altogether. The agreement is all fixed up and it will be signed in a couple of days. But if the creditors hear that a great wad of diamonds has turned up, they'll want to grab them to cover the rest of the debt. It wouldn't be human nature not to. After all, they'd be theirs morally as well as legally. D'you see?"

"I don't think so," replied Kerrigan cautiously. There was no point in appearing to be particularly intelligent.

Ilford was inclined to be impatient.

"I should have thought that it was as plain as a pikestaff," he exclaimed. "Don't go ferreting about for the diamonds until the day after tomorrow when the agreement is signed. That's what I'm driving at. If you were a brainy sort of chap I wouldn't mind so much. Brainy chaps have been on the game for a hundred years or so. But it's just your type of blithering fool that blunders on to a thing like this."

"Thank you very much," murmured Kerrigan.

"Don't try to be sarcastic with me," said Ilford simply. "I don't like sarcasm. And as I am about a foot taller than you are, and at least four stone heavier, I am in a very good position to enforce a certain amount of respect from you."

"But you have my respect without having to get it by force." Kerrigan tried to look nervous and frightened. Ilford took a step towards him, and said:

"You've got it clear, eh? No monkey-tricks now." Peter, sternly resisting the temptation to fetch the truculent baronet a quick punch in the middle of the waistcoat, asked meekly:

"What about Streatfield and his Jeeves?"

"His what?"

"His gentleman's personal gentleman. Tarzan. Mowgli. The Boston Tar-Baby. You know who I mean. How are you going to stop them going on with the hunt? Not to mention the thug who pipped off Rubin, and any counter-thugs that may have been supporting the late Rubin."

"All you need concern yourself with, sir," replied Ilford coldly, "is your own inaction. I can look after the rest without your kind assistance."

He marched towards the door and was just going out when Kerrigan tried a chance shot.

"Can you look after Mr Tollemache? He seems an inquisitive old bird."

The effect of this simple question was electrical. Sir George Ilford came striding back, his fist clenched, his face dark, and the veins throbbing on his forehead.

"What exactly do you mean by that?" he asked with dangerous quietness.

Kerrigan managed to work up a very passable imitation of a frightened giggle.

"Oh, as a matter of fact, of course," he stammered, "I didn't mean anything. It was just so funny to imagine poor old Tollemache standing up against you. That was all."

"Oh, I see. That was all, was it? Very well." He turned and went out again, leaving a thoughtful man behind him.

Presently Lady Caroline came back. She also had a thoughtful expression on her ancient countenance. "There are too many starters in this race," she observed, closing the door behind her.

"Yes, but we're odds-on favourites," replied Peter.

"I've forgotten what that means," replied Lady Caroline with a sigh. "It's nearly thirty years since I last went to the Derby."

"May I have the honour of escorting you to it next week?"

Her eyes lit up. "I might think of it. I might certainly think of it. 'Tough Egg' is favourite, I think you said?"

"It wasn't me who said that, Lady Caroline. It must have been someone else you were discussing it with."

"Silence, this instant. To business. Harry told me where the book is; he also told me that that nasty little art-collector had asked him the same question not half a minute earlier."

"Is the book in here?" exclaimed Kerrigan quickly.

"Yes. Harry says if it's anywhere it's here. We can look it up in the catalogue."

"Whew! That's a good job. Tollemache hasn't been back. Now it's our turn to hold the fortress."

The catalogue—a massive book with vellum cover and steel clasps—announced that "Samplers, the Claydon, Drawings of," resided habitually upon Shelf 61B., and Kerrigan put a step-ladder in front of Bookcase Number 61, and climbed up to Shelf B., Lady Caroline eagerly screaming instructions and advice from below. But "Samplers, the Claydon, Drawings of," was not upon Shelf B., nor upon any other shelf in Bookcase 61. Kerrigan descended the ladder and said, "That's that." Lady Caroline tapped her teeth with her lorgnette and replied, "It certainly would seem so."

"This requires long and careful thought," went on Peter. "Oh no, it doesn't," he added with sudden briskness. "It's as plain as a pikestaff. Everyone that has made a recent dart at the Treasure has gone for the samplers themselves; that is to say, they either did not know of the existence of the book—in which case they couldn't have taken it away—or else they knew it was already gone. But one gentleman had any amount of leisure in this library to find it and use it, and any amount of opportunity to take it away with him, and that is Mr Hone, ex-librarian. In fact, I shouldn't be surprised if it was the finding of that book that put him on to the scent in the beginning. In any case, after he had solved the problem he wasn't going to run the risk of anyone else finding the book, so he carted it away with him."

"Or else hid it somewhere else in the library," interrupted Lady Caroline.

"Or else, as you so shrewdly observe, Lady C., hid it somewhere else in the library. My own idea is that he would be more likely to get rid of it by the unobtrusive method of wrapping it in brown paper, affixing a stamp or two and bunging it into the out-going mailbag. In which case it may be anywhere, but might just possibly be still at Mr J. Hone's private residence, if he has one. In the meantime it's gone, and I must go too."

"In pursuit of that red-haired girl, eh?"

"Simply in the way of business, your ladyship," said Kerrigan with a bow.

"And how do you propose catching them?"

"It's going to be extremely difficult. But the blue of that Bentley is very vivid."

"You don't know that Rosemary girl at all well?"

"No, I'm afraid I don't."

"She won't miss the traceability of that blue. She'll make half a dozen changes of car before she lets them settle down in a quiet country hotel to work out the problem."

"It would be a bore for me if she succeeded," said Kerrigan, "but I don't see how it can affect you, Lady C. Presumably you'd have to hand over your three-quarters to the family chest."

"Presumably," said the old lady dryly, and again there was more than the suspicion of a wink in the venerable eyelid; "in any case, I'm not going to let Streatfield and that brat Pamela get away with it. Catch them putting it back into the family chest! They'd hang on to it and clear out to America or somewhere."

"Well," said Kerrigan, "I've got to get after them, and that right rapidly."

"There's just one other thing before you go," said Lady Caroline. "If you assume that this Treasure is as valuable as old Lord Claydon thought it was, and if you assume that although he wanted to hide it and make a practical joke of it, yet at the same time he didn't want it lost permanently, it is more than likely that he had several copies of his sampler-book made."

"More than likely," agreed Kerrigan.

"He might even have had it printed."

"As you say, he might even have had it printed. But as it's a hundred years ago, it's unlikely that we would find a copy upon the bookstalls."

"Most unlikely, Peter. But have you ever heard of the British Museum?"

"No. But I'm not surprised to hear that there is one. There was one at Petersburg. I never went into it myself, but I used to meet a girl outside it in the evenings at one time. That's how I come to know about it."

"I am not interested in your licentious past. Please don't refer to it again," said Lady Caroline severely. "Concentrate upon the British Museum."

"Consider me as concentrated exclusively upon the British Museum."

"Very well. It contains a library with a number of books in it."

"How many?"

"Several millions."

"Several millions! Whew! And if this book of drawings was printed, a copy of it might be there?"

"That was my idea. Anyway it's worth trying. Off you go to the Museum— I'll give you my admission-card—"

"Do you go there to read, Lady Caroline?" exclaimed Kerrigan in surprise.

"I haven't been inside the place for fifty years, but I belong to an Art Society that gets admission-tickets every year. In any case, they don't look very closely at the tickets. Anyone with a little assurance can walk straight in—and from the little I've seen of you, I should say that you've got a certain amount of assurance—and the catalogue man will look it up for you. If the book is there, you mayn't take it away with you, but you can copy out the quotations from *Hamlet* and bring them back here as quick as you can."

"But how the dickens shall I know which are from *Hamlet*, and which aren't?"

Lady Caroline tapped him sharply on the shoulder. "Copy them all out, then, you illiterate child. I suppose you know how to write?"

"Yes, and read."

"A monument of erudition. You can take my car."

"That reminds me. I've got a car hidden in a field quite close."

"Very well. Run along, now, run along!"

Peter Kerrigan ran along.

X

Warm Work at Chiswick

It is uncertain whether it was Lady Caroline's ticket of admission or Peter Kerrigan's naturally buoyant self-confidence that did the trick, but at any rate there was no difficulty about getting into the vast, book-filled dome. The young man halted abruptly on the threshold—and was sharply bumped from behind by a hurrying Afghan student who was poring over his book as he went instead of looking where he was going—and stared round him in astonishment. He had never been in such a room in his life; and he had seldom seen any people like the occupants who sat at desks, and buried their noses in gigantic piles of books. Kerrigan himself was no great reader, and the sight of a man or woman actually sitting down to tackle fifteen or twenty books simultaneously filled him with respectful awe. They were so superbly indifferent to their surroundings, so utterly oblivious of anything outside their piles of literature. Peter felt that if he pulled out a pistol and fired a shot through the glass roof nobody would pay the slightest attention. One or two of the readers might brush glass splinters off their desks, but most of them would not even hear the noise of the shot. Another reader—a Hindu this time—bumped into him, and this reminded him that he was blocking the gangway, so he advanced to the huge circular catalogue-counter and handed in his request. Twenty minutes later an assistant came back with a thin black book and handed it to him. It was called *The Claydon Samplers*, and on the fly-leaf there was an inscription recording the fact that it had been presented to the Museum by the Earl of Claydon in 1818.

Kerrigan eagerly took it to a desk and examined it. It consisted simply of the twenty-four engravings. There was not a single word of letterpress throughout, except the title of the book, and Kerrigan had to set to work to copy out the quotations on each of the twenty-four samplers. It took more than an hour to complete the job, and then, before returning to Marsh Manor, he drove to the house off Gower Street where the brother of the missing librarian lived, knocked, and asked for Mr Hone.

The little lecturer was at home, and he came shuffling to the door in tattered bedroom slippers and blinked at Kerrigan. He obviously did not recognise him.

Kerrigan greeted him heartily.

"Cheer up, Mr Hone. You look gloomy. Had your pocket picked again?"

"Oh, it's you, of course—silly of me—won't you come in? How are you?" said the little man with a rush.

"No, I've only a moment to spare. Any news of your brother?"

"Not a word. Not a line. Oh! It's too terrible! He's dead, I know he's dead—murdered just the same as those other poor fellows. It's horrible. And all because John was clever enough to find that way of making a million pounds."

"Steady, Mr Hone, steady. Keep calm. There's no proof that he's dead. He may be alive and kicking with the best of them."

"No, no, no!" wailed the little man. "The police keep on coming to me and asking me questions, and they've circulated everywhere and broadcast for him and put his photograph in the papers, but it's eight weeks now since he went away. Nobody could hide for eight weeks without being found. And not a word from him all this time!"

"Not even a parcel?"

"Oh yes, there was a parcel, but that was sent off before he disappeared— the day before—and the police came this morning and took that away."

Kerrigan's heart gave a bound. "They took it away this morning?"

"Yes, I don't know why. One of them came and asked if there had been a parcel. And of course I said yes, and gave it to him. I thought it was funny they didn't ask for it before if they've known about it all this time and wanted it."

"Was it a policeman in uniform who came for it?"

"No, a plain-clothes man. A detective."

"How did you know he was a detective?"

"He said he was," replied Mr Hone simply, and then added in a panic. "You don't think he was an impostor, do you? He couldn't have been an impostor surely?"

"Oh, I don't suppose so for a moment," said Kerrigan soothingly. "What did he look like?"

"Well, he was quite a young man with chubby pink cheeks and a very soft voice—now that you mention it, he didn't look at all like an ordinary policeman—and he spoke very pleasantly."

"No trace of an American accent?"

"Oh, none. I should have noticed that at once."

"And what was in the parcel, Mr Hone?"

"I don't know. I didn't open it. It was addressed by my brother to himself, you see, and there was a postcard asking me to keep it for him."

"Well," said Kerrigan, "if you'll take my advice, you'll telephone at once to Scotland Yard, ask for Inspector Fleming, and tell him about this young cherub with the soft voice. Fleming may be interested. If you like, you can mention my name. My name is—"

The lecturer interrupted with a pallid smile.

"I may have forgotten you just at first, Mr Carkeek, but I haven't forgotten you entirely you see."

"Oh, yes; quite, quite!" said Mr Carkeek, who was rather taken aback at the resurrection of his forgotten *nom de guerre*. "As a matter of fact, Fleming knows me better by my Christian name—Kerrigan is my Christian name."

"Kerrigan Carkeek," murmured little Mr Hone. "What a singular cacophony."

"It isn't my fault," replied Peter, who had not the faintest idea what cacophony meant. "And now run off and telephone to Fleming. It's urgent, vitally urgent:"

"It's all so bewildering, and so terrible," Mr Hone broke into a wail again. "I shall never see my poor brother again:"

"Very sad," thought Kerrigan, as he got into his car, "but devilish like the advertisement for Bovril." He drove to Piccadilly, parked his car in Wardour Street, and sauntered round to Orange Street, a small and dingy thoroughfare that runs off Leicester Square. He went into the entrance of a high, shabby-looking house, up a long, dark flight of stairs, and knocked at a battered door, labelled B. Smail.

The door was opened by a pale, spotty youth who announced firmly that Mr Smail was out and that no visitors were admitted.

"Rats to you!" observed Kerrigan genially, and raising his voice he shouted, "Ohé, Barney! Barney lad, let's in."

A shout came from the dark interior and was followed by a fat, heavy man with a big jowl and a huge unlit cigar gripped firmly in irregular, yellow teeth. "Why, Pete!" he cried, holding out a hand that felt like a slab of fish, "come right in, boy. I haven't seen you for the heck of a time. I've got Dutchy here, you know Dutchy? Hey, Dutchy, d'you know young Pete Kerrigan? Smartest lad in this or any other burg!"

He led the way into an inner sanctum where another fat, heavy man was sitting in an easy chair. His cigar, however, was in full blast.

Kerrigan knew him by name—"Dutchy" Goertz, a gentleman who had been prominent among receivers of stolen goods for many years in Barcelona, Marseilles, Rotterdam, and London—and shook hands with him cordially.

"I know you by name, Mr Goertz, and I'm sorry I haven't ever brought you anything in the way of business."

The fat receiver laughed, a deep guttural laugh. "And I know you by name, Mr Kerrigan, and if you brought me anything in the way of business, I wouldn't touch it. They tell me that you could work the three-card trick on a Sheffield racecourse gang and get away with it."

Kerrigan smiled modestly. "Praise from Mr Goertz is praise indeed," he remarked.

Mr Goertz backed away in mock alarm and buttoned up his coat. "Hands off!" he cried. "I haven't got any money on me."

"Well, young Pete," said Smail, "and what can I do for you? Sell you a packet of snow? Or would you prefer heroin?"

"Information—as usual, Barney," said Kerrigan. "Do you know a young fellow with initial D., pink chubby cheeks, and a very soft voice, and who makes about as much noise when he walks in the dark as a cat on a heap of cotton-wool, and is clever as a cartload of monkeys, and shoots plumb straight?" He addressed the question to Smail, but he turned sharply on Mr Goertz at the end of it, for that individual was undoubtedly shifting uneasily in his seat. Barney noticed it, too, and said, "Well, Dutchy, do you know him?"

"I know of him," admitted the other; and then, lowering his voice to a whisper, he said, "Hellish dangerous."

"Well," said Barney, "the description means nothing in my young life, but then I'm a specialist. I don't mix with people much outside the dope crowd. Dutchy's a mixer, and you can believe me, Peter, or you can believe me not, just as you please, but when Dutchy says a man is hellish dangerous you can lay a dollar or two that he's the wrong man to run a kindergarten. Come on, Dutchy; spill some more. We're all friends here."

"Your kid not listening at the door?" asked the cautious receiver. Barney shook his head.

"You see this little glass?" he said, jerking his thumb at a small square mirror that was fixed to the wall near his elbow, glass upwards. "If you look in here, you can see my outer room there. Periscope. Neat, eh? No, there isn't no one going to fool round Barney's keyhole. No, sir."

"Very good," said Goertz, "and if Barney will guarantee you, Mr Kerrigan, I'll tell you all I know about a man who answers to that description."

"Go ahead," said Mr Smail succinctly. "Pete's O.K."

"Well," said Goertz slowly, "there's a man called the Duke—no one knows his real name, but he's English right enough and he's a gentleman—who's made a trade for himself in America during the last ten or fifteen years. He's the Millionaires' Pet."

"Sounds harmless enough," said Kerrigan. "What does he do?"

"He'll do anything a millionaire pays him to do, and he won't blackmail him afterwards. That's how he's got his reputation—and his customers. If a man pays him to recover a document, say, that didn't ought to be drifting round the world, and the Duke recovers it, he hands it to his employer. He doesn't do what all the rest would do, use it to blackmail the fellow himself. He's got a regular scale of tariffs, and he'll undertake anything, provided it's for a millionaire, or a Corporation that can pay his scale. And that's about all I know. Your man may not be the same, but it sounds like the Duke."

"It sounds very like the Duke," murmured Kerrigan.

"Can you put me on to anyone who knows him personally?"

"No, by thunder, and I wouldn't if I could. If the Duke knew that I was putting anyone on to him, he'd soon plug a .45 into my anatomy, and I'm too old for that sort of thing. I tell you, he doesn't care two brass pins for any man's life except his own, and I should say he rated that at three brass pins."

"I take it, then, that you won't invite us to meet over a friendly cocktail?"

"No, sir, I will not," was the emphatic reply.

"What about you, Barney? Will you give me a hand?"

"Count me right out of this," answered the placid Mr Smail. "I'm one for peace at any price. I'm not a man of blood and iron."

Kerrigan rose. "Well, gentlemen, I am very much obliged to you for your information, so far as it goes. *Auf Wiedersehen.*"

The man called Dutchy Goertz heaved himself to his feet and held out his hand.

"Take my advice, lad," he said, "leave the Duke alone. He's the original, number one, hall-marked, twenty-two carat son of a gun. If you try to get him, he'll get you as sure as fate. So long, lad."

Kerrigan shook the two large flabby hands that were offered to him and went out. Half-way down the stairs he heard a soft footstep behind him and spun round. It was the fat receiver, coming down much more nimbly than his bulk seemed to allow for. The stairs were very dark and quite deserted save for the two men. As Goertz passed Kerrigan he said in a quick whisper, "Try 33 Rome Street," and went out of the building without a glance at the young man.

* * *

Peter Kerrigan was of an instinctively cautious disposition. If it was absolutely necessary, he could be as reckless as anyone, but he disliked and, to a certain degree despised, recklessness. He regarded it as being made up of 10 per cent bravery and 90 per cent folly. To him it was the same sort of quality that distinguishes the bull-dog. Kerrigan vastly preferred the calculating and far-seeing courage of the cat. He liked to take as few risks as possible and to be ready with a previously planned line of retreat in case the worst came to the worst. It was, therefore, only after a good deal of thought and preparation that he approached the dingy number thirty-three of the dingy Rome Street, that lies off a dingy Soho Square. He had paid a visit in the meantime to Clarkson's, the world-famous theatrical costumiers, and now resembled an elderly, grey-whiskered, and stoutish parson—complete with umbrella, books from the London Library on the classics, gloves, patched elastic-sided boots, and a look of mild harassment.

It took him half an hour to make his preliminary survey of the house, and at the end of that half-hour he had to admit that he had learnt nothing of the slightest interest or value. The house was exactly the same to all outward appearance as 31 or 35, or any others in the street. No one had either come in or gone out. No one had appeared at any window, no shadow had crossed any blind.

The reverend gentleman tried bolder measures. He took out a small packet of religious leaflets, with which Mr Clarkson's establishment, faithful as ever to its tradition of accuracy down to the smallest details, had provided him, and started to deliver them at each of the odd numbers in the street. He had to wait several minutes on the doorstep of Number 33 before there was any answer to his repeated knockings and ringing. Finally the door was opened by an old woman who might have been turned out of the same mould as any of the other old women in the street.

Kerrigan tried to detain her with conversation about parochial matters, but it was a subject about which she appeared to know even less than he did, and over which she certainly was not disposed to linger. But, looking past her into the hall he saw a telephone hanging beside the hat-rack, and a few moments later he discovered from the Supervisor that the number was Soho 1412, and the subscriber's name was Hood.

He then rang up the number and, when a woman's voice answered the phone, he said in a husky whisper that there was danger from a fat man disguised as a clergyman. The woman gasped, and whispered back: "But he's just been here."

Kerrigan had to make up his mind in a fraction of a second what line to pursue, and he decided to take the boldest.

"He's just turning down Rome Street," he said, "follow him." And he added, as a pressing afterthought, "But whatever you do, no violence," and he rang off.

Then pulling his clerical hat firmly down on his ears, and resisting the temptation to light an extremely unclerical cigar, he left the telephone-box and started off down Rome Street. The door of Number 33 opened as he passed, and someone—he dared not look round came out of the door and followed him. He had one unpleasant moment at the idea that it might be the redoubtable Duke himself who was upon his track, and that he might take the liberty of disregarding the telephone injunction to a Gandhi-like non-violence, but on the whole it was unlikely that anyone would be foolish enough to run the risk of gun-work in the West End of London, and Peter dodged through Soho out into Shaftesbury Avenue and got on to a bus. By securing a seat on the lower deck beside the door, he was able to watch for the pursuer without exciting any suspicion, and he turned towards the conductor an expression that was intended to convey an owl-like innocence. The only person who got on to the bus after him was a middle-aged man in a black coat and black trousers and a stiff collar and bowler hat. He carried a small dispatch-case and looked a very ordinary sort of business man. There was, however, a slight traffic block lower down Shaftesbury Avenue, and two young men got on to the bus who had a distinctly tough appearance. They wore soft hats and very smart grey flannel suits and shiny, pointed patent-leather shoes, and neither of them had shaved for several days. They addressed the conductor in American accents—booked ninepenny fares to the terminus of the journey, and incessantly picked their teeth with matches.

The middle-aged businessman immersed himself in his documents, the clergyman studied a prayer-book which he was not surprised to find had been supplied with his outfit, and the bus bowled gaily along to Hammersmith, Chiswick, and Acton Town.

Kerrigan was confident about the young men; he was a good deal less certain about the businessman whose mild attention seemed to be wholly devoted to his documents. In fact, his suspicions were based wholly on the facts that the man had undoubtedly followed him on to the bus and was undoubtedly making an unusually long journey. And even these suspicions were allayed when the man suddenly got off at Stamford Brook Underground Station and disappeared up a side street. By this time the two young men had produced a pack of cards and were passing the time cutting through the pack, and Kerrigan felt that he had by now memorised the details of their personal appearance with sufficient accuracy to be able to recognise them again, for certain, through any disguise. He wondered if they had done the same by him, as he dismounted from the bus and walked slowly along a side-street that led to Chiswick Mall. He had gained a little from his expedition if he had become familiar with the appearance of two of the Duke's assistants, and he had tested to a certain extent the accuracy of Dutchy Goertz's information about Number 33 Rome Street. But the man he was after was the Duke himself. There were two strong motives for running his head into what sounded like an exceedingly dangerous hornet's nest. Firstly, Kerrigan had no great faith in the capacity of himself and Lady Caroline to solve the problem of the samplers. He had never been much of a hand at such things, and he was fairly certain that his temporary and venerable colleague had enjoyed even less experience in this line; and even if they succeeded in solving the puzzle, it was more than likely that the redoubtable Duke—if indeed it was the Duke who had shot Rubin— would arrive at a solution much more quickly. There was, in fact, every chance that he had done so already. In any case, Kerrigan was convinced that his best chance lay in ignoring the cipher and striking straight at the Duke.

Secondly, and this was characteristically far-seeing of Kerrigan, it seemed as if the Duke might be a useful man to know for future occasions. He might offer to join him in partnership, or he might try to blackmail him, or to pick his pocket. There were lots of possibilities about a man like the Duke—even if he did sound a little dangerous—and Peter Kerrigan was determined to find him if it could be done without wasting too much time. And it looked as if there would be no necessity to waste a lot of time. The two shiny-shoed toughs now padding slowly down the road after him provided an excellent link with the Duke, and they had the air of men who would be quick workers if pushed to it.

An array of estate-agents' notice-boards on an empty warehouse which backed on to the river, caught Kerrigan's eye, and he slowed up and looked with a swift professional glance at the padlock which secured its heavy double door. It seemed to be an ordinary padlock, and a moment or two with a skeleton key proved that it was an ordinary padlock, and, had an inquisitive citizen of Chiswick happened to be watching at that moment, he would probably have been very surprised to see a stoutish parson disappearing into an empty warehouse and shooting a heavy bolt after him.

A quick glance round showed Kerrigan at once that he had fallen on his feet. The warehouse was exactly suited for his purpose. There was no window on the ground floor, and what little light there was came filtering through a broken trapdoor from the floor above. Peter ran nimbly up the wooden ladder and found that the second floor was illuminated by one grimy window overlooking the street and another, slightly less grimy, overlooking the river. Outside this second window there was a wooden platform and a rusty apparatus with iron wheels, chains, and ropes for loading and unloading boats. The whole place bore many signs of having been disused for a long time. Peter went out on to the platform and surveyed his surroundings.

Twenty yards away from the warehouse and separated from it by a narrow lane that ran down to the river's edge, stood a large house in a pleasantly large garden, a relic of old uncrowded days when London was fringed by large houses standing, dignified and aloof, in their own grounds. This survivor, though now jostled by warehouses and slums, still managed to preserve some of its dignity and aloofness, and the tastefulness of the layout of the garden and the absence of lace curtains in the windows seemed to indicate that it might be inhabited by people who would render assistance to the Church in distress. After making sure, therefore, that it was impossible for him to be overlooked from the street, and that no spy had as yet ventured down the narrow lane as far as the river, he lowered himself down the ropes into the water, dived, and swam under water as far as he could—cumbered as he was by his clothes and heavy boots. When at last he was forced to rise to the surface, he found that he had managed to pass the end of the lane and was out of sight from the main road. He dived again and came up at the end of the garden farthest from the warehouse. There were now enough trees and shrubs between him and any possible observers to make a safe landing, and a moment or two later he was standing, dripping, outside the back door. An excited and sympathetic maid rushed, gibbering incoherently, for an excited and sympathetic lady-of-the-house, and in an hour's time the Reverend Eustace Hardy was lying on a sofa in a comfortable drawing-room, clad in a pair of grey woollen pyjamas, a brown woollen dressing-gown, and a pair of woollen bed-socks. At his side was a table upon which stood a tall glass of hot whisky and water and lemon, for the Reverend Eustace had most lamentably caught a chill after his gallant dive into the river to save a drowning child. Lady Harrower, the lady-of-the-house, was in an ecstasy of mingled anxiety for the life of the brave cleric, admiration for his grey wavy hair and blue eyes, and delight at being able to entertain and succour a clergyman. She was a charming, fluttering, simple lady of about five-and-fifty, and as the Reverend Eustace drained his glass and held it out for a refill he congratulated himself upon his extraordinarily good luck.

Lady Harrower required no prompting to offer him a bed for the night, and only a little manœuvring was required to ensure that the bedroom faced the warehouse. From the bedroom window the reverend gentleman could see sentries in the road, and from a window in the passage he could see a small rowing-boat patrolling slowly up and down the river.

As soon as twilight began to fall, at about ten o'clock, Peter went out for a stroll in the garden, explaining to a twittering hostess that his chill had been entirely subdued by her aspirin and whisky, and that all he required was a little fresh air.

From a vantage point in a shrubbery he was able to watch the swift and methodical raid upon the empty warehouse at about a quarter to twelve. It was carried out by four men led by the quiet businessman who had travelled down in the bus from Shaftesbury Avenue. But there was no sign of anyone resembling the formidable Duke. He, apparently, did not do all the dirty work himself.

Early next morning, the Reverend Eustace parted with expressions of mutual goodwill from his benefactress and returned to Bicester.

XI

The Shakespeare Clues

The big blue Bentley car, gathering speed, vanished behind the trees, and a moment or two later the last sound of its powerful exhaust died away on the Bicester road. The occupants were in high good humour, and as the car swung out of the park gates, they simultaneously exploded in a peal of laughter. Even the grim Colombian servant laughed, showing his teeth like a hyena. Streatfield, who was driving, was the first to return to earth.

"What's the next move?" he asked.

Lady Pamela shrugged her elegant shoulders.

"I don't know," she replied. "Let's drive to Claridge's and do some thinking."

"Good egg!" said Streatfield. "We can also toy with a spot of dinner after we've solved the great mystery. I say, didn't we score off all that pack of blighters neatly?" He and Pamela laughed again.

Rosemary Shackleford looked thoughtful. "Doesn't it seem to you," she asked, "that they might be able to trace a car like this? After all, it is a little conspicuous, isn't it?"

"What does it matter if they do trace us?" replied Streatfield with a short laugh. "I fancy that Esteban and I could tackle Ilford or that insurance fellow if it came to a rough house."

"I wasn't thinking about them. I was thinking about the people who bumped off first Mr Newman and then Mr Rubin."

"I'm not much afraid of them either," said Streatfield. "I've seen some queer things and met some queer people in my time and it takes a good deal to worry me."

Lady Pamela looked admiringly at the brown, efficient face of her fiancé. Sitting half crouched over the wheel, his profile set and determined, driving with a combination of caution and brilliance, the captain certainly looked a difficult man to intimidate. But Rosemary seemed to be less impressed than Pamela.

"I don't see what you can do against gunmen," she argued, but Streatfield brushed aside the suggestion with a petulant shake of the head.

"Two can take a hand at gun-play," he said shortly, and Pamela added, "Don't be so absurd, Rosemary."

But Rosemary refused to be suppressed.

"Even if you are so confident about yourselves," she said, "speaking for myself, I have no desire to be hanging around if there's going to be gun-play. So just be good children and listen to me. In about half an hour we shall be at Great Missenden. You'll drop me there with all the samplers. I'll hire a car and dodge away across country until I find some nice country pub where I can settle down in quiet to solve the problem of the Treasure. You and Gerald and Esteban can go to Claridge's and shoot as many people as you like in the meantime. But if you take my advice you'll lie pretty low. The man who shot poor Mr Rubin doesn't strike me as being a man to try and be funny with. But that's just as you please," she added hastily, seeing that Streatfield was about to say something.

Lady Pamela answered instead.

"Why do you imagine, Rosemary, that you can solve the cipher or whatever it is by yourself? Don't you think three heads are better than one?"

Rosemary Shackleford smiled.

"Pam, darling, I love you dearly, but I never thought you were a genius."

Lady Pamela was obviously not very pleased at this frankness, but she replied:

"Well, what about Gerald?"

"Gerald and Esteban are the strong-arm squad," answered Rosemary with another smile. "Their business to distract the bullets from me while I'm doing the thinking."

"Rosemary, darling," expostulated Pamela, "what on earth are you talking about? Gerald is perfectly brilliant. Everyone knows that."

"Dear child, of course he is. I see I shall have to explain from the very beginning. Assuming that Mr Kerrigan was speaking the truth—"

"A pretty big assumption," growled Streatfield, "the beastly little counter-jumper!"

"No, Gerald," said Pamela unexpectedly, "I am pretty sure that he was telling the truth. He was much too frightened of you to do anything else."

"Permitting me to continue," went on Rosemary, as the big car slid through the village of Aston Clinton, famous as the home of one of the unfortunate Brides in the Bath, "assuming, as we must for the time being, that he was telling the truth, we have here in this car the clue which may lead us to a million pounds. There are several other people who know of the existence of this clue, and who know also that we've got it. It is fairly obvious that there will be a considerable hue and cry. People don't let a million pounds slip away quite so easily as all that. Now, we aren't a very difficult party to trace. We've got a rather ostentatious car; we've got Esteban, who looks as if he'd stepped straight out of Lord George Sanger's; we've got Gerald, who's got a cut across his face; we've got Lady Pamela Marsh, one of the most damnably be-photographed of England's brightest and youngest; and I've got red hair," she concluded. "What do you know about all that?"

"There's certainly something in that," conceded Streatfield. "What do you suggest?"

"That we split up, of course. I'll keep my hat well down over my vermillion tresses and dodge away with the samplers, while you scatter into London."

Streatfield swerved beautifully round a stray cow that was contemplating suicide in the middle of the road, and pursed his lips thoughtfully. Lady Pamela chipped in:

"In theory I think you're right, Rosemary. But in practice—er—well—"

"What's your trouble?"

"I'm not sure, darling, that you're the right person to do the dodging away and puzzling out of the cipher. I think Gerald would be better at it."

"Pamela!" exclaimed Rosemary, "I never heard such nonsense. Of course I'd be better at it. Besides, Gerald's scar is much harder to hide than my hair!"

"I don't think I would be very good," said Streatfield. "I never pretended to be able to solve that sort of thing. I'm better at practical things."

"You see, Pamela darling?"

Lady Pamela's pretty pink-and-white face clouded over dangerously, and she said in a cold, unpleasant voice:

"You must remember, Rosemary, that this million pounds belongs to my family and not to yours." Rosemary Shackleford flushed.

"In that case, I'll drop out of it at once. Will you stop, please, Gerald? I can easily walk to a garage and hire a car home."

"Don't be idiotic!" said Streatfield. "Pam, you're a fool. You've got no brains, nor have I. Rosemary's chock-a-block with them. We can't do without her, even if we wanted to. And so far as I'm concerned, we don't want to."

Pamela laid her hand on the other girl's sleeve. "Don't be angry with me, darling. I'm all worked up about the whole thing. My nerves are all to hell. Of course you're the one to slip away with the samplers. Forget everything I said."

Streatfield interposed tactfully.

"We're just coming to Tring, Rosemary. I suggest that you stop here and raise a car."

"If you're sure you want me to."

"Absolutely," they both replied.

"Very well. Pull up now, Gerald. I'll walk into the village. I mustn't appear in this car."

Streatfield pulled up, and Rosemary, the samplers under her arm, got out.

"I'll ring up Claridge's when I've found a place. But for Heaven's sake be careful. You'll be watched all the time."

"Oh, we'll be careful," said Streatfield dryly. "Don't worry about us. Good luck. Cheerio!"

Rosemary walked into Tring, hired a car, and was driven to Amersham, where she paid it off and hired another car to Maidenhead. At Maidenhead a motorbus took her to Slough, and a third hired car finally deposited her at half-past eight that evening at a small country inn in Surrey, situated near the village of Churt, and named the Pride of the Valley. She engaged a room, dined in a shaded corner of the dining-room, and kept her hat on during the meal, and after dinner retired to the seclusion of her room to study the twenty-four samplers which had adorned the walls of the mad Lord Claydon's library.

At half-past eleven she retired to bed without having advanced one inch towards a solution, and after breakfast next day she started again. Rosemary had never before realised how exhausting brain-work can be. By lunchtime she was quite worn out, and she spent the afternoon recovering some of her mental energy by strolling on the Surrey commons.

That same morning Peter Kerrigan returned to Marsh Manor with the results of his expedition to London, which he laid before Lady Caroline. The old lady was extremely annoyed at his delay in returning, and reprimanded him for his quite unnecessary escapade at Chiswick.

"You might have been killed!" she exclaimed at him in high, piercing tones. "The Lord knows the world would be a better place if you had been, and no one would have cared two straws about it. But I want your help to get this money. Do you understand? After I've got it you can do what you like. But until then no more nonsense."

"I wanted to find the man who shot Rubin," protested Kerrigan.

"Why? What was your idea? What do you mean?"

"I thought if I went into partnership with him," said Peter with a grin, "he might not speak to me like a Prussian sergeant-major."

"Young man," said Lady Caroline, "as soon as we've got this money, I shall do my level best to get you hanged!"

"Nobody as gracious as you could be so cruel," retorted Peter.

"Give me those Shakespeare quotations," said the old lady austerely, and Kerrigan laid on the table the results of his hour in the reading-room of the

Museum. Lady Caroline sorted out the six slips marked *Hamlet*, and put the others aside.

"Now," she said grimly. "What about it?" She stared at them and Kerrigan stared at them. Then she asked sharply. "These numbers in the corners—were they on the samplers?"

"Yes. Each set was numbered one to six."

"Then we'd better put them in that order." She rearranged the slips in order, and the quotations, all in blue wool, except one in red, ran as follows:

On Number 1, three lines:

"With all my love I do commend me to him."
"My lord, you shall tell us where the body is."
"But, see, where sadly the poor wretch comes reading."

On Number 2, three lines:

"For to that sleep of death what dreams may come."
"The passion ending, doth its purpose lose."
"And marshal me to knavery. Let it stand."

On Number 3, three lines:

"Or but a sickly part in one true sense."
"Behind this arras I'll convey myself."
(In red wool):
"Is not this a swift fellow, my lord? he's as good at anything and yet not a fool:"

On Number 4, three lines:

"Hath this man no feeling of his business?"
"Within the book and folio of my brain."
"To pay four ducats, four, I would not farm it."

On Number 5, three lines:

"I pray thee, pass with your best violence."
"Most lazar-like with foul and loathsome crust:"
"With evil speeches of his father's death."

On Number 6, three lines:

> "For if the sun breed decay in a dead dog."
> "With thoughts beyond the reaches in our souls."
> "In mine impudence, your skill shall, like a star."

After several minutes of complete silence, Lady Caroline said slowly and thoughtfully:

"What an extraordinary collection of quotations! Let me look at the others." She scrutinised carefully the slips on which Kerrigan had copied out the quotations from *Macbeth*, *Othello*, and *Lear*, and then returned to the *Hamlet* slips. "The first thing which jumps to the eye is very obvious, isn't it?"

Kerrigan looked at her doubtfully. He was rather out of his depth.

"Oh, of course," she went on impatiently, "you're illiterate, I forgot. I'll explain, if possible in words of one syllable. There are a lot of well-known quotations in all of Shakespeare's plays. In these three sets"—she pointed to the slips from *Macbeth*, *Othello*, and *Lear*—"the quotations are almost all well known. But not one of the *Hamlet* ones is even remotely well known."

"Perhaps," ventured Kerrigan unwisely, "*Hamlet* doesn't contain so many well-known ones as the others," and he instantly regretted his rashness in the withering sneer with which the suggestion was greeted.

"These quotations from *Hamlet*," went on Lady Caroline, "are not only not well known; many of them are not worth quoting. 'Behind this arras I'll convey myself,' or 'With all my love I do commend me to him.' It's absurd to spend days sewing rubbish like that on to a sampler. That proves conclusively that we're right in concentrating on the *Hamlet* samplers. The famous quotations are put in as a blind; these have been chosen because they contain the words or letters or something which makes the cipher."

"Why is one of the lines sewn in red wool when all the others are sewn in blue?" observed Kerrigan thoughtfully.

"Which one? Oh yes. 'Is not this a swift fellow, my lord? He's as good at anything and yet not a fool.' H'm! If it's the only one that is sewn in red, there must be some reason for it. It must be the key to the cipher."

"Or else it's been done in red simply to make us think that it's the key."

"Let's assume it's the key," said Lady Caroline, and together they wrestled with the problem unavailingly until lunchtime. They tried anagrams and alternative words and every third word and every fourth word and initial letters and last letters and every conceivable combination of words and letters and syllables. But it was all in vain. They utterly failed to extract an iota of sense from the samplers.

Luncheon was not a very cheerful meal. Lord Claydon and Sir George Ilford did not appear. The only other guest at the table was Mr Tollemache, and, as Lady Caroline refused to open her mouth except to put food into it, and was completely lost in thought, the burden of entertaining Mr Tollemache fell entirely upon Kerrigan.

The art-valuer seemed to be obsessed with the famous Treasure. He talked of nothing else.

"It may be an epoch in the History of Art, Mr Kerrigan," he kept on saying. "It may mean nothing less than the disclosing of some of the great lost pictures. It may lead to a new chapter in the history of the world."

"Pictures easy things to hide?" asked Kerrigan with his mouth full of cold salmon.

"Oh no, oh no," chirruped Mr Tollemache. "That I grant you. That I concede you frankly. They are not easy things to hide. Rolled up, they are tolerably bulky, and unrolled they often cover a widish space. But it is possible, my dear sir, surely you will admit that it is possible that the old Lord Claydon was such a clever man that he found a hiding-place that baffled generations of searchers."

"It's possible, of course."

"Now what are your views, Mr Kerrigan? What do you think of the chances of finding the famous Treasure? In your experience, Mr Kerrigan, you must have come across cases of pictures being lost or stolen and turning up in very queer places?"

"What exactly do you mean by my experience?" inquired Kerrigan guardedly.

"In your work for your Insurance Company."

Kerrigan had forgotten that he had recently adopted that profession for a short time.

"Ah yes? But my line has been life insurance. Not works of art."

Mr Tollemache was disappointed, and the conversation languished. After luncheon Lady Caroline took Kerrigan aside.

"I am now going to take a nap," she announced. "I want you to get a copy of *Hamlet* from the library, read it through until you come to the quotation that is sewn in red upon the third sampler, and have the place ready for me at half-past three when I wake up. The context may give us some clue."

Kerrigan set about his novel task with considerable interest. It was a quite new experience for him, and he always enjoyed anything that was new. He found a copy of *Hamlet* and, selecting a corner of the library that commanded all the windows and the two doors, he built himself a rampart out of the *Encyclopedia Britannica*, laid a pistol on the desk beside him, and set to work.

Peter Kerrigan paid no attention whatsoever to omens or superstitions, but he paid a good deal of attention to the possibility of being taken by surprise.

He was soon absorbed in *Hamlet*, and his emotions as he read were mingled admiration, puzzlement, and amusement. The notion of killing a man by pouring poison in his ear struck him as extremely ingenious; on the other hand, he could not understand the scruples of a man who would not bump off his hated enemy simply because he found him praying. Hamlet's device of ensuring that Rosencrantz and Guilderstern would be put on the spot as soon as they arrived in England appealed to him; and Polonius seemed to be simply asking for trouble by hiding behind a curtain and spying. He found the language at times difficult to understand and he profoundly despised Hamlet's indecision. On the other hand he was immensely awed by what he called Shakespeare's "gift of the gab"; a fellow who could reel off words like that was obviously a learned sort of card, a university professor most likely or a barrister; at any rate, a fellow who lived in a library. Ophelia and her lamentable fortunes almost brought tears to his eyes, while the king's treachery in the last scene made him angry.

But of the line which was sewn in red upon Sampler No. 3 of the series he could find no trace. To make quite certain he read the whole play through again. The line was not there. There was, however, one line which seemed vaguely familiar, and that was the very last line in the play: "Go bid the soldiers shoot," and it took him at least ten minutes of brain-cudgelling before he remembered that it was the inexplicable postscript to the letter from John Hone to his brother which had started all the trouble. "Go bid the soldiers shoot, eh, old chap?" had been the words. That was something, at any rate. The whole assumption from the beginning had been that John Hone had solved the cipher and felt that his hand lay upon the Treasure. And here, in his triumphant letter to his brother, he had quoted Hamlet in a jubilant postscript.

Surely that was an additional confirmation that the secret lay in the *Hamlet* samplers. And yet the first line that he had tried to trace in *Hamlet* was not there! As it was not quite half-past three, the hour of Lady Caroline's awakening from her siesta, Kerrigan set himself to try and trace another of the quotations, and very soon ran to earth Line 2 on Sampler Two: "The passion ending, doth the purpose lose."

He tried again, and found Line 1, Sampler Three: "Or but a sickly part of one true sense." Then Lady Caroline appeared, and he handed her his results. She was keenly interested.

"The only line in red is not in Hamlet," she repeated several times. "That's extraordinarily interesting. That makes me more certain than ever that it's the key to the whole cipher. Peter, we've got to get that line!" She closed her eyes and murmured, "'Is not this a swift fellow, my lord? He's as good at anything and yet not a fool.' It's familiar, Peter, it's very familiar, and yet somehow it's not familiar. It doesn't sound right. It's got something queer about it."

"We've got to hurry up about it," said Peter half to himself. "We haven't got much time."

Lady Caroline looked at him waspishly.

"Your part in this affair is to make time for me," she said. "You've got to keep the world out of this library until I've solved the cipher. That's all you're good for."

"Let me remind your ladyship," said Kerrigan blandly, "that although I am a match, on the average, for ten ordinary men, I fancy that in a short time I may be called upon to cope with one extraordinary man backed by about twenty ordinary ones."

But Lady Caroline was not listening. Her eyes were shut and she was murmuring, "Is not this a swift fellow, my lord?"

Then she opened her eyes and said sharply:

"Get me Christ Church College, Oxford, on the telephone, and ask for Professor Macnamara."

Bicester is no great distance from Oxford; the telephone service was in its blandest mood and the Professor chanced to be in college, so the call did not take more than twenty minutes to put through. Lady Caroline seized the receiver, announced herself, and exchanged brief greetings. Then she said:

"Professor, I am trying to run to earth a quotation and I want your help. Listen carefully while I repeat it." She gave the quotation twice, slowly and clearly, and then there was a pause. She repeated it a third time, and then the Professor gave his verdict. Lady Caroline thanked him, replaced the receiver, and turned to Kerrigan.

"It's a misquotation," she announced, from *As You Like It*, Act v. Scene iv."

"From as I like what?" inquired Kerrigan, mystified.

"Another of Shakespeare's plays," the old lady said impatiently. "Really, you are the most ignorant young man I've ever met! The old Lord Claydon who built this library would have positively hated you. He hated his own children because they were so ignorant. The quotation ought to be "Is not this a rare fellow, my lord?' You see? 'Rare' instead of 'swift.' Pass me over the Shakespeare."

She turned up *As You Like It* and read aloud the words, and then the dialogue that led up to and succeeded the words, and then shook her head. "There doesn't seem much to help us there."

"But why should anyone make a mistake in the quotation?" demanded Peter, his wits thoroughly roused. "If it was written, a mistake wouldn't be so bad; it would be understandable. But to go and solemnly sew the wrong word, and to sew it in the wrong colour, and to choose the quotation from the wrong play—it couldn't possibly have been an accident. It's out of the question."

"You're right, Peter. Of course you are. It's intentionally wrong, and the red wool is to draw our attention to it."

"Perhaps 'rare' is some sort of key-word?"

"Either 'rare' or 'swift.'"

"The trouble about key-words," said Kerrigan, "is that there are dozens of different ways in which a key-word can be used."

"I suppose," replied Lady Caroline, "there are experts in ciphers whom we could hire to solve it. But I've no idea how we can lay our hands upon one. Perhaps that is the sort of thing that you are good at—finding professional cipher experts?"

"I suppose," said Kerrigan slowly, "that there are such things, but I wonder very much if it's that sort of cipher."

"What's your idea?"

"I was thinking about the mad old Lord Claydon," he answered. "I don't suppose he wanted the Treasure to be lost permanently, and so he wouldn't have made the cipher too difficult. There may be professional solvers nowadays, but I don't imagine that they existed prominently in the 'twenties or 'thirties."

"Well!" said Lady Caroline sharply. "What are you driving at?"

"The old man was fond of cruel practical jokes; he also hated the laziness and ignorance of his children and his nephews and so on. How would it be if he invented this story of the Treasure, and left these Shakespeare clues simply in order to make them all study Shakespeare?"

"And the Treasure would be the intimate knowledge of Shakespeare that they would gain in doing so?"

"Don't you think that's possible?"

"I think it's very possible. I think it's damnably possible!" exclaimed the old lady with spirit. "It's exactly the sort of thing he would have enjoyed." She paused, and then went on again. "There are one or two arguments against it, though, I'm glad to say. So far as we can make out, only the *Hamlet* samplers are to be used. That means that his children would only have had to study one play, whereas with a little more trouble he could have made them study lots of the plays. And if there's no Treasure, what was it that John Hone found?"

"Yes, there's something in that." Kerrigan brightened. "He obviously found something. Then here's another idea. There was a Treasure, a real one, and old man Claydon—"

"Old Lord Claydon, if you please," corrected Lady Caroline sharply. "He was my great-grand-uncle!"

"Old Lord Claydon hid it so that the finder of it at least had to wade through one play of Shakespeare's to find it. He was rewarded for his trouble, and the others were scored off for their ignorance. How about that?"

"I sincerely hope that is the correct view," replied the old lady, "and I propose that we act as if it was. In other words, we must study our *Hamlet*."

"Keeping in mind the application of a key-word which is either 'swift' or 'rare.'"

"It might be that as 'swift' has been substituted for 'rare' we are to substitute 's' for 'r,' 'w' for 'a,' 'i' for the next 'r,' 'f' for 'e,' 't' for the next 'r,' and so on."

It did not take long for this theory to fall to the ground.

"In any case," pointed out Kerrigan, "we aren't studying *Hamlet*. We aren't improving our minds." But Lady Caroline was not listening. She was examining Slip No. 6 most intently through her lorgnettes.

"'In mine impudence, your skill shall, like a star,'" she muttered. "Why 'in impudence'?"

"It struck me, Lady C.," replied Kerrigan, "that Gaffer Shakespeare is a bit obscure from time to time; of course, I'm not a judge—"

"Exactly!" she snapped. "On the other hand, I am. In my days girls were educated. William Shakespeare never wrote 'in mine impudence.' It's ridiculous! Find the passage in *Hamlet* where he says that."

"Dash it all!" protested Kerrigan. "I've already read it all through twice. Have I got to plug through it all again?"

"You're learning your *Hamlet*," said the old lady grimly. "Just as if you were a descendant of old man Claydon."

With an exaggerated sigh, Kerrigan sorted out the play from the other volumes and started to skim through it rapidly, in search of the words, "In mine impudence—" Lady Caroline went on studying the slips through her lorgnettes, and for a time there was silence.

After a few minutes Kerrigan looked up.

"I've come across the first one of all. Sampler No. 1, line 1: 'With all my love I do commend me to you.' Don't you think while I'm about it we might note down where to find each of them? It will save time in the long run. It's in Act I., Scene v., line 184."

Lady Caroline jotted it down.

A little later Kerrigan read out: "'But look, where sadly the poor wretch comes reading.' Act II., Scene ii., line 167," and Lady Caroline duly made a note of it, and then a moment afterwards: "and here's the one about the sun and the dead dog, same Act and Scene, line 180."

The next one was: "'For in that sleep of death what dreams may come,' Act III., Scene i., line 67, and the next: 'The passion ending, doth the purpose lose.' Act III., Scene ii., line 207, and the next: 'Behind the arras I'll convey myself,' Act III., Scene iii., line 28."

It was not until Kerrigan was half-way through Act IV. that Lady Caroline pulled him up sharply. He had just said:

"Here's another: Act IV., Scene iv., line 20. 'To pay five ducats, five, I would not farm it.'"

"Four ducats, four, you mean," interrupted Lady Caroline.

"No, madam, I mean five ducats, five."

"Then it's another mistake." They stared at each other until Lady Caroline said quietly: "Go on, Peter. Just find that one about 'impudence.'"

Kerrigan had to read almost to the end of the play before he found Hamlet's words: "I'll be your foil, Laertes; in mine ignorance your skill shall, like a star i' the darkest night, stick fiery off indeed."

"A singular capacity for making mistakes," observed Lady Caroline dryly, "Let us start all over again." They started all over again and examined each quotation carefully; Kerrigan finding them in the book and Lady Caroline checking them on the slips and jotting them down on a large sheet of paper, writing the line from the slip first and the same line, as Kerrigan found it in the book, immediately after it. The result was curious. Lady Caroline's sheet ran as follows:

Slip 1. "With all my love I do commend me to him."
Book. "With all my love I do commend me to *you*."
Slip. "My lord, you shall tell us where the body is."
Book. "My lord, *must* shall tell us where the body is."
Slip. "But see, where sadly the poor wretch comes reading."
Book. "But *look*, where sadly the poor wretch comes reading."
Slip 2. "For to that sleep of death what dreams may come."
Book. "For *in* that sleep of death what dreams may come."
Slip. "The passion ending, doth its purpose lose."
Book. "The passion ending, doth *the* purpose lose."
Slip. "And marshal me to knavery. Let it stand:"
Book. "And marshal me to knavery. Let it *work*:"
Slip 3. "Or but a sickly part in our true sense."
Book. "Or but a sickly part *of* our true sense."
Slip. "Behind this arras I'll convey myself."
Book. "Behind *the* arras I'll convey myself."

Then came the quotation from *As You Like It*, when the word "swift" was substituted for the word "rare." Then:

Slip 4. "Hath this man no feeling of his business."
Book. "Hath this *fellow* no feeling of his business."
Slip. "Within the book and folio of my brain."
Book. "Within the book and *volume* of my brain."
Slip. "To pay four ducats, four, I would not farm
Book. Slip. "To pay *five* ducats, *five*, I would not farm
Slip 5. "I pray thee, pass with your best violence."
Book. "I pray *you*, pass with your best violence."
Slip. "Most lazar-like with foul and loathsome crust."
Book. "Most lazar-like with *vile* and loathsome crust."
Slip. "With evil speeches of his father's death."
Book. "With *pestilent* speeches of his father's death."
Slip 6. "For if the sun breed decay in a dead dog."
Book. "For if the sun breed *maggots* in a dead dog."
Slip. "With thoughts beyond the reaches in our souls."
Book. "With thoughts beyond the reaches *of* our souls."
Slip. "In mine impudence, your skill shall, like a star."
Book. "In mine *ignorance*, your skill shall, like a star."

"Well," said Kerrigan, mopping his brow with an elegant silk handkerchief, "I don't know what happened to Lord Claydon's children, but I think I can repeat that infernal play word for word, and I don't care two straws if I never hear of it again, or of Brother Shakespeare either. What do you make of it, Lady C.? Where do we stand? Have we got our hands upon a million dollars—our pickers and stealers upon the ducats? Damnation! I'm beginning to quote that stuff already."

"I've got as far as this," replied Lady Caroline coolly. "The words which ought to have been in the samplers but weren't, read as follows: 'You must look in the work of the rare fellow volume five you vile pestilent maggots of ignorance.'"

XII

The Third Murder

"That's all very well," said Kerrigan. "That's all jolly clever and nice. But who is the rare fellow? Is it Gaffer Shakespeare himself?"

"No, I don't think so," replied Lady Caroline. "I rather fancy it must be intended for Ben Jonson. Don't ask foolish questions," she went on hastily. "Ben Jonson was a poet and a playwright, and on his memorial stone in Westminster Abbey, it says, 'O rare Ben Jonson!'"

Kerrigan gazed at the old lady in respectful admiration.

"What an awful lot you do know," he said. "Let's try and find this sportsman's literary work. Jonson, Benjamin. You sit there, Lady C., while I look round for it."

In about a quarter of an hour he found the complete works of that illustrious writer, and inside the cover of Volume V. there was a pocket, consisting simply of a flap of paper which had been pasted on to the board. The pocket was empty.

"I was afraid of that," murmured Lady Caroline, her eyes fixed abstractedly upon the work. "That man Hone got it, of course."

"Yes, but what did he do with it? That's the point."

"And a very curious point it is, too," replied her ladyship; "very curious indeed."

Kerrigan examined the book again carefully. "There couldn't have been very much in here," he said. "It's too small to hold more than a couple of sheets of notepaper."

"It obviously held a piece of paper with the instructions for finding the Treasure; probably another of these cipher jokes. That's clear enough. What isn't so obvious is why Hone ran the risk of taking it away with him when we're more or less agreed that he left the Treasure behind. It seems silly, and yet the man couldn't have been very silly or he wouldn't have got as far as this. You see, Peter, or at least you will see after I've explained it to you, there was first of all the clues on the samplers. Hone didn't take them away—"

"Perhaps they were a bit too bulky to march out with under his arm."

"Don't interrupt. He only had to take the one with the line in red on it. The word 'rare' is the vital word."

"That's true:"

"Thank you," said Lady Caroline icily. "Very well. He leaves the first clue, and he leaves the Treasure; but he takes the second clue away with him. That doesn't sound reasonable:"

"Perhaps he's hidden it."

"Of course he's hidden it. He must have. And that brings us up against a very pretty little problem. He must have hidden it in the obvious place— slipped it into any one of the ten thousand books which are lying on the shelves of this library. The next thing for you to do is to find it."

"That will take a goodish bit of time," said Peter dubiously.

"Not if we employ the local troop of Boy Scouts and offer a handsome reward for the discovery of a document!"

"He may have memorised it and then burnt it."

"Of course he may. But we've got to assume that he hasn't! Go down and find the local scoutmaster and fix it up with him."

Peter Kerrigan took his car and drove into Bicester in search of scouts. His first port of call was the Angel Hotel. Not only did it sell admirable beer, but, like all inns, it was a centre of information. Kerrigan was just polishing off a tankard of ale when he became aware that a man was sitting in a dark corner of the lounge, half-hidden by an aspidistra, watching him. The next moment he had slid into the chair beside the man and was saying:

"Dear old Inspector Fleming! Revisiting your ancient haunts? What will you have? Landlord, a good deal of ale at your earliest convenience."

"Well, Mr Kerrigan," replied Fleming calmly, "so you're still hanging around? Have you found that million pounds?"

"No. Have you found that murderer?"

Fleming smiled. "The police have a clue," he said. "Tell me, have you been bothered with any more Treasure-hunting strangers at Marsh Manor?"

"No. The place has been comparatively free of them lately. I was beginning to wonder what had happened to them all. Do you suppose that the man who shot Rubin got away with it after all?"

"You mean the Duke?" asked Fleming casually. Kerrigan started. "Don't look so surprised, Mr Kerrigan," went on the detective, pulling out a pipe and beginning to fill it. "You aren't the only person who can find things out."

"You're an old fox!" said Kerrigan admiringly. "I always said you were. What else do you know?" But Fleming was too busy lighting his pipe to answer the question. The next time he did speak, he observed:

"It's been a curious case in one or two ways. Chicago gangsters so seldom bring their feuds over here. It's interesting to see their methods at work. They are different in several ways from the methods of our bad eggs."

"In what sort of way?"

"Well, they're much more reckless for one thing. In Chicago they're accustomed to shooting people in the streets and getting away with it, and they've got the idea that they can do the same thing when they come to other countries. It makes them take all kinds of absurd risks. On the other hand"— Fleming paused and then went on seriously—"on the other hand, Kerrigan, I'm flabbergasted at the technical skill of some of them. I had no idea the thing could be carried to such a pitch. That business in the library over there when Rubin was shot was a bit of an eye-opener for me, I can tell you. I wasn't thirty yards away, in that little room at the end of the library with the door open, and I didn't hear a sound until Rubin came in from the house. The other fellow came in from the garden without a sound."

"A remarkable feat," said Kerrigan, adding with a modest cough, "I know how difficult it was because I had just done it myself."

Fleming laughed. "But then I'm never surprised at any talents for villainy that you display, my dear fellow. And, incidentally, you'll admit that the Duke made a brilliant get-away. The whole thing was a masterpiece from beginning to end."

"How did you tumble to the fact that it was the Duke?"

"That was easy once the Chicago police identified Newman as one of his pals."

"And have you caught him yet?"

"Not yet," replied Fleming quietly. "But it's only a matter of hours."

"Have you tried 33 Rome Street, Soho?"

"We raided it after your visit to it yesterday."

Kerrigan sat bolt upright. "Say that again slowly." Fleming smiled indulgently.

"Surely you knew that we would—er—follow you about a little, Kerrigan. You're such a knowing young fellow."

"You infernal old fox!" cried Kerrigan.

"You looked a most benign parson. I would have joined your congregation at once if I'd thought you had got a church. You see, Kerrigan, you've got crooked ways of finding things out quickly that I haven't got. I've no doubt that it would have taken me as long as forty-eight hours, or perhaps even more, to get as far as the Rome Street house. By having you watched, we got there in six hours. Very simple, isn't it?"

"Then you saw that business down in Chiswick?"

"And very neat and clever I thought it was. We scooped in all five of the lads who went into the warehouse. They were all Yanks. They'll come up tomorrow on 'feloniously entering,' 'illegal possession of firearms,' and perhaps on 'loitering with intent to commit.' Remanded, of course, for a fortnight." Kerrigan became indignant.

"Do you mean to tell me that you, my boyhood's chum, deliberately allowed six murderous thugs to follow me into a disused warehouse at dead of night, loaded up with gatlings and stuffed eelskins? Why didn't you clap them into irons before they went in? You had no means of knowing that I wasn't inside. In my opinion, you're a cold-blooded, callous, hardhearted policeman!"

Fleming laughed gently.

"Sergeant Maitland was very worried about it," he said. "He felt very strongly about it and said that it wasn't right or fair."

"Sergeant Maitland is a good citizen."

"Yes, but he's very soft-hearted. And he really was worried about those six fellows. He kept on saying that no doubt they were stiffs, and thugs, and hooligans, and probably kicked their grandmothers, and robbed orphans, but after all, he was a humane man and fair was fair, and it wasn't right to let them run such a frightful risk."

"Sergeant Maitland ought to be sunk in mid-channel with a stone round his neck."

"But I pointed out to him," continued Fleming blandly, "that you were certain to have cleared out long ago, and were probably at that very moment picking a pocket in Leicester Square or selling a goldbrick to an Australian in the lounge of the First Avenue Hotel in Holborn."

Kerrigan got up and surveyed the detective coldly. "Your idea of quiet, gentlemanly fun," he said, "is not my idea of quiet, gentlemanly fun, and I dislike your taste in conversation. Furthermore"—he broke off and stared at a man who came into the hotel at that moment "furthermore," he repeated absurdly, and his voice trailed away and he sat down again abruptly and pulled out his pocket-book; he rummaged in it and produced a photograph which he glanced at and handed to Fleming. Fleming looked from the photograph to the stranger and back again at the photograph. Then he handed it back, nodded, and raised his eyebrows in inquiry.

Kerrigan got up and yawned.

"What about a game of billiards? There's a table in there."

He led the way into the billiard-room. As soon as the door closed behind them, he said in a quick whisper:

"That's Hone, the librarian who disappeared." Fleming's brows contracted and his eyes shone, but he said only "Ah!" and then he slowly relit his pipe—a totally unnecessary waste of a match, as the pipe was already in full blast. Then:

"So that's Hone," he observed very thoughtfully. "That's exceedingly interesting. I think I would like a talk with him."

"Half a minute!" exclaimed Kerrigan. "Don't be hasty. What do you want to talk to him about?"

"About the present whereabouts of the Duke. I fancy he might be able to tell us a thing or two."

"I should think nothing was more unlikely," replied Kerrigan emphatically. "I don't see how he could possibly know anything. And if you go and talk to him, you'll only make him frightened and you'll get nothing out of him at all. Whereas if you leave him alone—"

"He'll lead you to the Treasure!" interrupted Fleming dryly.

"Damnation!" exclaimed Kerrigan. "I wish I'd never told you who he is."

Fleming inserted a forefinger into the young man's buttonhole and said to him in a kindly voice:

"Look here, Kerrigan, if you can find that Treasure you're welcome to it so far as I'm concerned. But don't go and run unnecessary risks. So long as the Duke is at large you'll be in danger. If you help me to rope him in, then you'll have a clear field for treasure-hunting and you can go ahead. But at present you haven't got a clear field."

"Just leave him alone for this one evening," begged Kerrigan. "After that you can do what you like."

"It isn't worth while taking the risk," replied Fleming firmly.

"Risk be damned! The Duke won't come near Bicester again after killing a man within a couple of miles of the place two days ago."

"That's exactly what I think he will do," replied Fleming quietly, "and that's why I'm here. Come on; there's no time to waste."

He led the way into the lounge again and walked across to where Hone was talking in an undertone to the landlord.

"Mr Hone, I think?" he began, and the ex-librarian spun round, his face white and his lips trembling. "You've made a mistake," he stammered, but Fleming patted him soothingly on the arm. "It's quite all right," he said. "Come into the billiard-room and have a talk. I'm a police inspector from Scotland Yard." Hone stumbled twice before he reached the billiard-room, and he was obviously in a pitiable state of nerves. "Now," said Fleming, shutting the door, "this is my friend, Mr Kerrigan. Get him a drink, Kerrigan. You can speak just as freely in front of him as in front of me. I want to know all you can tell me about the man who is called the Duke?"

Hone shivered violently at the mention of this young gentleman's pseudonym, and for a moment or two he found it difficult to utter an intelligible sound. At last he managed to say in a low voice:

"I had something for sale, and he got me kidnapped. He threatened me with torture. I had to tell him part of the secret. I didn't tell him the whole secret. Then I escaped. If I hadn't, he would have tortured me when he got back and found that I hadn't told him the whole of it."

"You told him about the samplers?" asked Kerrigan. Hone turned an eye that contained a bloodshot mixture of terror and low cunning upon him.

"Yes, I told him that the Treasure was sewn into the back of one of the samplers. I had to invent something. It was the best I could do. There was a red-hot poker in front of my nose."

"And where is he now?" asked Fleming sharply. Hone shrugged his shoulders.

"I haven't the faintest idea." He drank off a neat brandy at a gulp and a little colour came into his cheeks.

"Where were you kidnapped to?"

"A house in St John's Wood. I think I could find it again. It was near Marlborough Road Underground Station."

"We'll start for St John's Wood in five minutes," said Fleming. Hone started abruptly.

"I can't go back there—I daren't go back there! He would kill me!" The man's voice rose to a pitiable wail.

"Don't be absurd," said Fleming. "You'll be surrounded by dozens of policemen. How could he possibly get at you? Besides, I very much doubt if he's still there."

Hone seemed a little reassured by this, and his spirits rose slightly, especially when Kerrigan brought him another drink.

"You swear I'll be protected?"

"Of course you'll be protected. All you've got to do is to identify the house and then you can do what you like."

"There's just one thing, Inspector." Hone had a sudden relapse into his nervous fit and began stammering again. "A very small matter. I left Marsh Manor rather abruptly some six or seven weeks ago and I—er—I—er had to leave a good deal of my baggage behind me. Would it be very inconvenient if I hired a car and went to Marsh Manor now and collected some of it? It wouldn't take me long. And then we could go to London afterwards."

"A very good suggestion," said Kerrigan warmly. "In fact, I'm going that way myself and I'll be very glad to drive you there."

Fleming frowned. He did not want to put unnecessary spokes in Kerrigan's wheel, but at the same time his paramount duty was to discover and raid the St John's Wood lair of the American murderer at the earliest possible moment.

"It's on the way to Aylesbury," went on Kerrigan. "You'll have to go by train from Aylesbury if you want to get up to London quickly. There aren't any good trains from here at this hour of the day."

This was a pure guess of Kerrigan's, but it turned out from an inspection of time-tables that it was substantially correct.

"All right," conceded Fleming reluctantly, "we'll stop at the Manor, but you must drive us to Aylesbury, Kerrigan."

"You bet I will! Come on, lads. What sort of luggage is it, Mr Hone? Books, I suppose? You librarians are great ones for books."

Hone seemed pleased with this suggestion, and Kerrigan guessed that the reason was that the ex-librarian had been looking for a plausible excuse for going into the library.

"Yes, as a matter of fact, yes," he replied jerkily. "As it happens I left several of my own books in the library. I should be glad to have them back."

Peter Kerrigan's spirits began to rise. It began to look as if the quest of the famous Treasure was really coming to a successful conclusion. He had started it as a mild amusement without any high hopes of profit, but had gradually got bitten with the undying fascination of all treasure-hunts, and, quite apart from the prospect of heavy financial gain, he was thoroughly excited at the possibility of succeeding where so many had failed. All he had to do now was to make certain that Hone was left for a few minutes alone in the library and then subsequently relieve him of any pocketbook, package, or parcel that he might be encumbered with. Or, simpler still, he might be able to hide in the library before Hone came in, and then pounce upon him red-handed, so to speak.

He reckoned, however, as Fleming had done before, without the resourcefulness of the redoubtable Duke. For, a mile out of Bicester, a powerful motor-bicycle came up from behind and the rider shot the unfortunate librarian neatly through the forehead, punctured the off-front tyre with another shot and disappeared round the next corner at sixty or seventy miles an hour. Half an hour later, while Fleming was making half the telephone wires in the country red-hot from Marsh Manor, Kerrigan walked into the library and found Rosemary Shackleford standing there with the fifth volume of Jonson's works in her hand.

XIII

Blackmail

Rosemary gave a faint start and coloured a little, but otherwise showed no sort of embarrassment.

"Good evening," she remarked quietly; "I was wondering if you would still be here."

"Good evening," replied Kerrigan gaily. "Doing a spot of quiet reading, eh?"

"It isn't often one gets a chance," Rosemary answered easily, replacing the volume of Jonson in the bookcase with an assumed casualness, and pulling out at random another book. "A queer jumble of stuff in here," she went on. "A lot of awful trash, and some good stuff as well."

"What about those samplers?" asked Peter bluntly. "Did you solve the mystery?"

The girl laughed.

"No, it was too much for me altogether. I'm no good at that sort of thing. Are you a cipher expert, Mr Kerrigan?"

"Good lord, no!"

"I should have thought you might be good at something," she said with mocking gaiety, "but it's difficult to find out what it is. It certainly isn't picquet, and it doesn't seem to be brain-work. What is your line, Mr Kerrigan? Basket-making? Fret-saw?"

"Professional boxing," replied Kerrigan, with a bow. There was a dry laugh from the doorway as Streatfield came in.

"Professional boxing!" he said. "I used to do a bit of boxing myself once. We might have a spar together some time."

Kerrigan assumed an air of nervousness.

"Oh, well! I'm not sure about that; I'm rather out of practice."

"Yes, I thought you might be," answered Streatfield with a laugh. "Pamela!" he called over his shoulder, "here's your young pal again!"

Lady Pamela came in and looked coldly at Kerrigan. Then she turned to Streatfield and said:

"We can't get rid of him so long as Aunt Caroline is here."

"Then I suggest," replied Streatfield, "that you put a little pressure upon your esteemed papa to get rid of Aunt Caroline."

Kerrigan replied affably: "I don't see why we shouldn't all be friends," but his eyes were not upon the pair he was addressing but upon Rosemary Shackleford. She was perched upon a desk, swinging one leg idly and gazing thoughtfully at the ground. He knew exactly what she was pondering about— the whereabouts of the piece of paper which had been in the Jonson volume. She struck him as being an exceedingly intelligent young lady. The pair who did all the talking and bluffing were simply ludicrous; but the tall, red-haired girl was quite different. He wondered what she was in the business for at all; he wondered if she really liked the bad-tempered and silly Lady Pamela; if she was trying to smooth the path of true love or if she was playing her own hand; if she was detachable from her present alliance or not. The last idea struck him as being worth while verifying. The trouble was that he himself could not verify it without disclosing that he knew a great deal more than he pretended, and Peter instinctively hated doing this. It was one of his strongest weapons in his incessant warfare with the world that people invariably underestimated him until it was too late. At the present moment he flattered himself that everyone in this present case underestimated him profoundly, and the most dangerous of them all, the Duke, did not even know of his existence.

He determined, therefore, to get Lady Caroline to try and detach Rosemary Shackleford from her present alliance. Without her, Lady Pamela and her offensive fiancé would be useless; with her, they kept on obstructing and getting in the way, and wasting time just at a critical juncture when time was of the utmost value. He nodded to Streatfield, bowed to the two girls and, remarking, "Well, I must go and lie down; I'm always so tired if I don't get an hour's rest in the evening," he strolled out in search of Lady Caroline.

As he drifted from room to room in his search, he could not help admitting to himself that the activities of the young gentleman who called himself the Duke were becoming a little alarming. The man was an obvious master of the Chicago technique of committing a murder in broad daylight and getting away with it. Of course, he could not conceivably continue to commit these daylight murders in England with impunity. Indeed, his luck had already been phenomenal. But the knowledge that he was still at large and apparently still undaunted by the police pursuit, by the broadcast descriptions, by the rewards and the photographs, by the mobilisation of the immensely efficient resources of British detection, was definitely disquieting. The man might easily make a final raid on Marsh Manor, and Kerrigan was certain that the police, even the quietly astute Fleming himself, would leave this possibility out of their calculations. They had no experience of the aggressive criminal. The Scotland Yard idea of a murderer was a man who, after committing his crime, ran away in a wild, overpowering panic, and hid in a clumsy amateurish fashion until in ninety-five cases out of a hundred he was caught and convicted. The murderer who took the offensive instead of bolting, who was as cool as a cucumber instead of being panic-stricken, and, most important of all, was no amateur at his job but a highly-skilled professional, was a phenomenon quite outside their experience and calculations. Kerrigan, reaching this point in his meditations, called a halt in his search for Lady Caroline until he had gone up to his room to get his pair of neat little black automatic pistols. With men like the Duke about the place, it was just as well to be armed and ready. Even that queer-looking Colombian servant would be more respectful in an emergency if he found himself at the business end of one of those pistols. Normally, Kerrigan relied on his own quickness and a length of gas-piping to carry him through the ordinary rough-and-tumble of life in a quiet country like England. But if Chicago methods were going to be introduced, they would have to be met by Chicago methods. The only trouble was that when he reached his room he found that the lock of his suitcase had been clumsily forced, and that his neat little black automatic pistols had vanished.

Peter Kerrigan sat down on his bed, lit a Russian cigarette, and put in some hard thinking. There was one vitally important question which had to be solved somehow or other at the earliest possible moment, and that was: did the thief break open the suitcase in order to disarm Kerrigan, or did he break open the suitcase to find something else and simply appropriate the pistols as a by-product, so to speak?

If the former, then somebody knew that he was a dangerous fellow, a man who was liable to have pistols in his luggage and who ought to be deprived of those pistols at an early date. If the latter, the position was not nearly so serious. It might mean an ordinary sneak-thief, or someone who wanted to make certain that Kerrigan was not masquerading, or someone who was examining all the luggage in the house. In the event of it being one of these three types of thief, the mere discovery of a pair of pistols would not necessarily lead to the deduction that he, Kerrigan, was a formidable individual. It might just as easily mean that he was panic-stricken at the idea of living in a house where two murders had recently been committed and had laid in an arsenal for the purpose of self-protection.

The identity of the thief was at present undiscoverable. Kerrigan had no finger-print apparatus nor microscope, nor indeed any technical detective skill. All he could do was to wait and see, and, in the meantime, use every means possible to replace his lost weapons. That was more than ever vitally important now that it was almost certain that there were active enemies inside the house as well as outside. He went downstairs and unobtrusively slipped into the gunroom to investigate the possibilities there. All the shot-guns and rook-rifles which had adorned the walls of the gun-room had vanished.

It was an extremely thoughtful Kerrigan who walked slowly down the long corridor towards the telephone, and before he had reached the instrument he had decided not to use it. There were too many chances of being overheard, and he was particularly anxious that the gentleman who had rifled his suit-case should not know that he was already aware of the theft and fully on his guard.

To purchase a firearm of some kind at a gunsmith's either in Bicester or in Aylesbury would involve the necessity of obtaining a gun-licence from the police and, although he was fairly ignorant of the workings of the British police on its routine, civil side, he was pretty confident that a local gendarmerie would be unlikely to hand over a gun-licence at a moment's notice to a total stranger who was not even a resident in the district. It might be possible to slip out and drive to a telephone-box and ask Barney Smail to send a gun down by special messenger. On the other hand, the entire district for miles round would already be seething with detectives and policemen, and it was any odds that every telephone call would be tapped and docketed and the sender traced; some zealous country bobby might easily clap him into the local stocks and keep him there all night before Fleming could arrive to bail him out. And it would be utterly impossible to leave Lady Caroline to cope with a possible inrush of thugs and gunmen during the night. There was no alternative but to do the best he could without firearms, and it was in rather a gloomy frame of mind for one who was by nature so buoyant, that he entered one of the smaller sitting-rooms and found a regular family row in progress. Lord Claydon, Lady Caroline Marsh, and Sir George Ilford were all talking simultaneously, rather loudly, and all three were indulging in small but vehement gesticulations. Had Peter Kerrigan been, a perfect gentlemen, the fine flower of Eton and Trinity, he would have backed out of the room with a mumbled apology. Had he been a thick-skinned counter-jumper, he would have pretended to notice nothing and would have advanced brazenly towards the vociferating group. But being, as he was, somewhere between the two, he stood in the doorway and watched the trio with unfeigned interest.

The two men stopped at once and stared at him, but Lady Caroline only glanced over her shoulder and went straight on, through a chorus of hisses and "hushes," in her high-pitched voice, "Publish and be damned. Publish and be damned."

"Will you stop your infernal squawking?" shouted Lord Claydon. It was the first time that Kerrigan had seen him display any vigorous emotion. He was red in the face and perspiring.

"I will not stop my infernal squawking," retorted the old lady with spirit. "I'm squawking for your good, as you very well know! It's the only sensible thing to do. Come in, Peter Kerrigan, and don't stand there like a street-boy watching a dog-fight."

Sir George Ilford's deep voice chimed in:

"If you say a word in front of that young sweep—"

"Yes?" snapped Lady Caroline. "Yes, George Ilford? And what will happen if I do?"

"I'll break his neck."

"And be hanged for your pains, and a good job, too. Don't you see, you pair of great fools, that you've got no other course open? Either you publish and be damned, or you use violence. There's no third course. Will you come into this room, Peter Kerrigan, or must I come for you and haul you in by the ears?"

Kerrigan advanced slowly, keeping an eye alert for the enormous baronet, whose scowling face and clenched fists added but little to the charm of his formidable appearance.

"Mr Kerrigan is now my secretary and colleague," went on Lady Caroline. "Did you get the Boy Scouts?"

"No, I didn't. There has been a certain amount of activity on the Western Front since I set out boy-scouting, so to speak."

"Well, I haven't time to listen to all that now. I want to tell you what's going on here."

"You'll do nothing of the kind!" shouted Lord Claydon, and Ilford exclaimed, "A dirty little tout!"

"He's never heard of Shakespeare," replied Lady Caroline sharply, "but he's a first-class hand at everything else. And he's my secretary, and if I mayn't consult my own secretary, who the devil may I consult? Yes, George, I said 'Who the devil,' and I mean 'Who the devil'!"

"Do you seriously propose, Caroline," asked Lord Claydon, "to admit a total stranger into my family secrets?"

"Not all of them, you fool."

Lord Claydon did not appear to be a man of great stamina. He had shot his bolt, and with a gesture of despair he sat down on a sofa. Sir George Ilford looked at him for a moment and then at the indomitable old lady, and then said, more calmly:

"I suppose if your mind is made up to tell him, nothing will stop you."

"Nothing!" she replied, with a sort of grim cheerfulness. Ilford shrugged his massive shoulders and walked over to the window.

"Peter!" went on Lady Caroline in a rapid undertone, "it's like this. That damnable old Mr Tollemache is the biggest and most poisonous blackmailer in the world."

Kerrigan gaped.

"That inoffensive old fish!" he exclaimed. "I thought he was an authenticated, all-square-and-above-board art-valuer and collector!"

"So he is. He's a collector all right. Only he does most of his collecting by blackmail. He's genuinely crazy about Art and Old Masters and that sort of thing, and as he never has any money to buy them with, he hit upon this simpler method of getting hold of them."

"And he's got something against Lord Claydon?" inquired Kerrigan. Lady Caroline nodded.

"I see. Yes, that explains a good deal," went on the young man thoughtfully. "He was going to exchange the incriminating documents for the pick of these Old Masters, and then he suddenly heard that we were all hot on the track of the famous Treasure, and he's holding off on the chance that he may be able to add that to the bag. Is that it?"

"There are a lot of things which might be said against you," observed Lady Caroline, "but no one could say that your mind works slowly."

"So, of course, Lord Claydon doesn't want the Treasure found just yet awhile," said Kerrigan.

Lord Claydon said nothing, but George Ilford answered for him.

"We've got to the end of our tether. We've told Tollemache that unless he accepts the original bargain—the documents against the pictures—by tomorrow evening, we'll tell him to go to hell."

"I wish you'd tell him to go to hell now," said Lady Caroline pugnaciously.

Lord Claydon mumbled, "No, no, no."

"Very well," said Kerrigan, "I see where we stand. We've got to postpone finding the Treasure until tomorrow for fear that Tollemache may scoop it. And we've got to find it at the earliest possible moment for fear that the Duke may scoop it. It's a pretty problem."

"The so-called Duke," said Ilford, "hasn't much of a chance. Half the police in England are after him. He'll be too occupied in looking after his own skin to worry any more about the Treasure."

"He managed to spare the time," replied Kerrigan quietly, "to murder John Hone a mile from here about half an hour ago."

The other three were stricken into an appalled and half-incredulous silence, broken at last by Lord Claydon, who said vaguely:

"John Hone? My librarian that was?"

"Yes. The man who started all this trouble by deciphering the first clue and hiding the second clue:"

"Murdered! But why?" Lord Claydon seemed utterly befogged.

"Because he was coming back to collar the Treasure."

Sir George Ilford spoke, and it was noticeable that for the first time he addressed Kerrigan as if he was a social equal:

"Then you think this Duke fellow may have another go at the house tonight?"

"I've no idea of what his plans are, or are likely to be. He's obviously a man of astonishing nerve."

"Then what do you advise?" Kerrigan heroically did not allow himself even the suggestion of a smile at the change in the baronet's tone.

"It isn't only the Duke we've got to reckon with," he observed. "I'm not sure that I care for this fellow Streatfield."

"Streatfield!" exclaimed Lord Claydon, arousing himself from his lethargy. "The fellow's going to marry Pamela. He's as straight as a die."

"You can be as straight as a die and still be fond of a million pounds."

"But do you mean to suggest that he and Pamela would walk off with the thing if they found it?"

"I think they might dish out a small share of it all round, but I fancy that Streatfield would find it difficult to part with the bulk of it."

"I simply don't believe you," asseverated Lord Claydon. "Besides, neither he nor Pamela have got the brains to find it."

"No. But that red-haired girl has," replied Kerrigan. "She's got as far as we have already."

"What!" shrilled Lady Caroline. "Rosemary Shackleford has got as far as Ben Jonson?"

"She has. She's reached Volume Five of his immortal works."

Lady Caroline calmed down suddenly into a stern grimness.

"So that in your opinion it's become a triple problem, eh? Tollemache, the Duke, and Streatfield," asked Ilford.

"Yes. And I think that you, Lady Caroline, could knock out the Streatfield party, if you could get hold of the Shackleford girl. Couldn't you see her and persuade her to come over to our side? Put all the cards on the table. Tell her the whole story. Streatfield will be absolutely useless without her."

"I refuse to believe," reiterated Lord Claydon, "that my daughter is capable of behaving in the slightest degree badly towards me. She knows that I'm in financial straits, and she wouldn't hesitate to stand by me."

"Quite so," said Lady Caroline dryly. "But we might just as well be on the safe side, and take no risks."

"The point is," said Ilford, "what are we to do?"

"Have you a pistol?" asked Kerrigan suddenly.

"Yes. In my room upstairs. Why?"

"Will you lend it to me?"

Ilford stared at him suspiciously. "Most certainly not."

"I wish you would," said Kerrigan.

"I expect you do. But I'm not such a half-witted fool as you seem to think." He marched to the door and went out.

Kerrigan turned to Lady Caroline.

"Will you try and detach that girl from Streatfield? It would save one complication if you could manage it. Things are difficult enough as they are:"

"Certainly, I'll try."

"Even if you fail, find out why she's so keen on helping Streatfield. Find out what their idea is. Find out—"

"I'll find out everything there is to know," she replied emphatically. "In the meantime, what about that second clue?"

"We're no worse off than anyone else with the possible exception of the Duke. He may have extracted its whereabouts from Hone. But Streatfield is no nearer than we are, and Tollemache isn't so near. The real danger is another of the Duke's dashing raids. The man is really rather superb, you know."

The door opened noisily and Ilford strode in; his dark face was darker than ever, and he was breathing heavily. He went straight up to Kerrigan.

"I say!" he exclaimed, "my room's been burgled, and my pistol's gone!"

"Ah!" murmured the other softly, "whoever it is, he's a thorough sort of worker. When did you see it last?"

"I don't know when I saw it last, but I know that my room hadn't been burgled this afternoon after lunch when I went up to get a handkerchief. It's in a damnable mess now."

"Where was the pistol?"

"In a drawer of the dressing-table."

"Loaded?"

"Yes."

"Well," said Kerrigan, "there's no point in taking any unnecessary risks. I'm going to ring up the Chief Constable of the county and get in touch with my friend Fleming. I've got the impression that things are likely to start moving this evening after dark. Lady Caroline, perhaps you would have the kindness to go and see Miss Shackleford. Sir George, not a word about your pistol. We're in deep waters. We've got to go carefully."

"Yes, but who took it?"

"I don't know, but I strongly suspect my friend Tarzan, the pride of Colombia."

"Streatfield's man?"

"Yes."

"I won't listen to a word against Streatfield," said Lord Claydon. "He's going to marry my daughter, Pamela."

No one paid any attention to him, and Kerrigan went off to telephone to London. Five minutes later he was seated in a big chair in the hall, once again thinking hard—for the telephone was out of order.

"It's only two miles to Bicester," he murmured, "but the man who cut the wire knows that as well as I do, so the road will be neatly ambushed between us and that admirable burg. Now, whatever am I to do?"

XIV

A Game of Poker

Of all the people inside the walls of Marsh Manor that evening, only Peter Kerrigan knew the full implications and possibilities of the situation. Of the rest, each knew a certain amount about the activities and intentions of some of the others, but only he was fully aware of the hidden dangers which surrounded the house from without and threatened it from within.

But although he was so alive to the situation, he was completely in the dark as to what, if anything, was likely to happen, and what he ought to do. The most menacing danger was unquestionably from the Duke; the most annoying was the fear that Streatfield and his melodramatic Colombian would make fools of themselves and start shooting; the most subtle attack would undoubtedly come from Mr Tollemache. Mr Tollemache was a new factor in the situation, and a rather disturbing factor. A man who had amassed a very large fortune from blackmail was obviously a man to be watched, not because he would be liable to a sudden violence, but because he must be a man of patient, far-seeing intelligence. He was a man of brains, whereas the Duke was a man of brilliant action, and Streatfield a man of clumsy forcefulness. Tollemache was certainly a man to watch. It was, of course, very difficult to estimate just how much he knew. For example, did he suspect Kerrigan to be more than an ordinary police-spy or a journalist? It was of great importance to know whether he underestimated his capacity. Streatfield unquestionably underestimated him, and the Duke did not know of his existence. The attitude of Tollemache had to be discovered, and Kerrigan decided to set about discovering it at once.

The art-valuer was sitting in the billiard-room, wearing a purple velvet jacket and an ancient pair of black baggy trousers and bedroom slippers, studying the current number of the *Burlington Magazine*. He looked up benignly as Kerrigan came in, and laid down the periodical.

"Ah! my young friend, come in, come in—I've had no one to talk to all day. Come and have a chat before we go off to dress for dinner. It is only seven o'clock:"

Kerrigan sat down and picked up the *Burlington* with a grimace.

"Rather outside my line of country," he said. "I'm afraid I'm not a very brainy sort of chap."

"I suppose you have to be very quick at figures in the insurance business," replied Mr Tollemache. "Everyone has a speciality. Yours is figures, mine is art. You wouldn't be able to detect a first-class forgery of a picture. I wouldn't be able to add up a column of figures correctly. Would you care for a game of billiards? I am but an indifferent performer."

"So am I," replied Kerrigan, "but I would be delighted to play."

At a quarter to eight Mr Tollemache was leading by forty-two points to thirty-nine; the highest break on either side having been seven, which included a fluke, and Kerrigan, as he went up to dress for dinner, admitted that he had learnt nothing whatever about him.

In the corridor outside his room he found Streatfield in earnest conversation with his villainous-looking Colombian servant.

"Hullo, Streatfield," he said genially; "having a heart-to-heart talk with the missing link? What's doing in the tree-tops, Mowgli? Everything all serene and jolly?"

They paid no attention to him beyond a couple of sour glances, and Streatfield went on talking in swift South American Spanish. Kerrigan pretended that his door was locked, and searched his pockets for the key.

"At eleven o'clock sharp," Streatfield was saying, "and have the car ready by the back gate of the park. And mind, no shooting unless it's absolutely essential."

"So they, at any rate, have not lost their guns," thought Kerrigan as he went into his room. A moment later there was a knock at the door and Lady Caroline came in. Her lips were tightly closed and her whole expression was one of stern annoyance.

"It's no good," she said; "she won't leave them."

"What's her idea?"

"Her idea," replied Lady Caroline in a tone which made it very obvious what she thought of Rosemary Shackleford, "is to stand by Pamela and her young man."

"And do you mean to say that Lady Pamela is out to rob her own father?"

"That is exactly what it amounts to."

"Dear me!" said Kerrigan; "I was under the impression that I knew a thing or two about tough circles, but I haven't often met charming young ladies who want to rob their papas."

"It's all that young man," snapped Lady Caroline. "I've met the type before. He's one of the ambitious kind. Not content with a hundred thousand pounds—must have a million. And that suits Pamela down to the ground. She's a girl who likes a good time and doesn't mind who has to pay for it so long as she gets it. And that Shackleford girl is her best friend and is going to stand by her."

"Oh, well, it doesn't really matter," replied Kerrigan. "The immediate and pressing danger is not from her brains; it's more from other folks' guns. After dinner tonight, Lady C., you've got to retire to your room and lock yourself in. We can't have you getting in the way of bullets."

"I shall do exactly what I choose, young man."

"No, really," begged Kerrigan. "I must ask you to keep out of the way tonight. I shall have my hands full enough as it is, without having to worry about you."

"Never mind about me; I can look after myself. And now I must go and dress for dinner." Lady Caroline paused at the door. "What do you really think is likely to happen? Anything at all?"

"Quite possibly nothing at all. It all depends on whether the Duke knows where to look for that second clue. If he does, he may make a desperate dash for it. And then things will move. If he doesn't, quite possibly nothing at all may happen. Personally, I think he'll turn up."

"And what are you going to do if he does?"

"I shall hang around and wait for what old man Shakespeare would probably have called a spot of inspiration."

"He would have called it nothing of the sort," said Lady Caroline severely.

* * *

Kerrigan was first down into the drawing-room before dinner, and he had already refused a cocktail before the next-comer, Rosemary Shackleford, appeared. He never touched alcohol if there was the prospect of a wild night before him. It was one of his few rules in life. Miss Shackleford took a glass from the tray and drained it at one gulp.

"No cocktail for you, Mr Kerrigan?" she inquired.

"I've already had three," he answered, with a very fine imitation of a self-conscious giggle, "and, to tell you the truth, I'm not really very accustomed to such strong drinks. At home I only have a little beer now and then."

"Three already! Do have another and see what happens!"

Kerrigan with another giggle took a glass and held it up to the light and then laid it on the window-sill. "I shall go all funny," he said, "but never mind. Eat and drink, for tomorrow we die, eh?"

The girl started a little at the peculiar aptness of the quotation and looked suspiciously at him. His face betrayed no emotion except a beaming and all-embracing geniality.

The next moment Streatfield came in quietly, and she turned to speak to him. With a swift movement Kerrigan threw the contents of his glass out of the window and lifted the glass to his lips as if he had just drained it off.

"I say, I say!" he exclaimed, spluttering a little, and coughing. "You were quite right, Miss Shackleford. Quite right. I needed just one more. I say, how right you were! How marvellously and beautifully right! What a marvellously and beautifully right person you are!"

As he spoke he intercepted a swift glance which passed between the other two. Streatfield replied smoothly:

"I am glad you find Miss Shackleford's advice good. I have been known to take it myself, sometimes."

"Streatfield, old chap," said Kerrigan. "You are an exceptionally wise and splendid fellow! I admire you a very great deal. Do you mind my admiring you a very great deal? You're so efficient and competent. I wish I was efficient and competent."

"I always admire efficiency," murmured a soft voice at the door as Mr Tollemache came quietly in, and the conversation became more or less general. Kerrigan talked incessantly for about ten minutes, and then pretended to get sleepy. It gave him a natural and reasonable opportunity for watching the others. During dinner, Rosemary, Pamela, and Streatfield drank a good deal, Sir George Ilford even more, and Lord Claydon hardly paused in the steady succession of glasses of wine which he poured down his throat. Mr Tollemache drank water, and Lady Caroline a single whisky and soda.

After dinner Kerrigan pretended to fall asleep on a sofa and only woke up when a game of poker was suggested by Streatfield. In an hour he had managed to lose thirty-four pounds, mainly to Lady Pamela, whose spirits rose proportionately. At half-past ten the game fizzled out in the face of a heavy series of ostentatious yawns from Streatfield, and the party began to break up for the night. Before anyone actually left the drawing-room, however, Streatfield turned to Lord Claydon and said:

"What about locking-up? Would you like me to give you a hand?"

Lord Claydon jumped eagerly at the offer and, with Sir George Ilford, set out for a tour of the house, locking, bolting, shuttering, and barring.

Lady Caroline retired to her room, Lady Pamela drifted out, Mr Tollemache had vanished some time ago, and Kerrigan was left alone with Rosemary. She went across to him and whispered, "Mr Kerrigan!"

"Eh?" he blinked, and half-stifled a yawn.

"Don't talk too loud. I want to tell you something." Kerrigan concealed the alertness with which he was listening.

"Well?" he drawled.

"It's about Lady Caroline," she murmured, "I want to help her without hurting poor Pamela, and I think I know how to do it."

"Help her! I didn't know she wanted help. In what sort of way?"

"Never mind about that. Will you take a message from me to her?"

"Yes."

"Then tell her to look in the wooden box at the foot of the cellar stairs," and with that the red-haired girl turned on her heel and went out.

Kerrigan had to act quickly. If he sat on the sofa and considered the position for more than five seconds, the girl would know that his suspicions were aroused and that, therefore, he was a man to be carefully watched. He jumped up and, singing softly but un-melodiously, walked unsteadily to the door and up the stairs. As he went, he saw, over the balustrade, the party of three who were locking up the house. They seemed to be making a thorough job of it.

He knocked at Lady Caroline's door and was admitted. The old lady was sitting bolt upright in a wooden chair studying an Italian grammar; she listened with interest to the message and, at the end, said emphatically:

"I thought that girl would come round. It wouldn't be in human nature to back Pamela against her father. Run down to the cellar and investigate, Peter, and come back here at once."

Kerrigan resumed his slightly swaying progress, descended the stairs, and drifted off in the direction of the entrance to the cellar. The big iron door at the top of the cellar stairs was open—apparently the locking-up party had not reached that part of the house—and, with a quick glance to make sure that he was unobserved, he slipped through and went down. The stairway was only illuminated by the light from the corridor above, and after its first right-angle twist it became difficult to see more than a yard or two. At the foot there was a second iron door, also part of the mad Lord Claydon's legacy to his posterity, and Kerrigan pushed it open and went in. He switched on an electric torch and surveyed his surroundings. The cellar was large and empty, save for a pile of old furniture heaped in one corner. The huge safe stood against the far wall—its door wide open—and beside it lay a wooden packing-case. Beyond the safe a blank opening led to an inner cellar. Kerrigan paused to listen and then, hearing no sound, advanced to the packing-case. It was quite empty, and just as he had satisfied himself that there was nothing in it or under it, he heard the cellar door shut with a snap and the sound of bolts being shot and footsteps faintly receding up the stairs.

"Stung!" he remarked aloud. "Very badly stung indeed."

It was characteristic of him that he spent no time cursing or regretting or kicking himself. He had made two bad mistakes in thinking that the girl

Rosemary had underestimated him and in underestimating her himself; and the only thing to do was to set about retrieving the position at the earliest possible moment. The first thing, obviously, was to explore the inner cellar, and he made for the black oblong which marked the entrance to it. But as he reached the entrance he got a really nasty shock, for a voice with a palpable American accent observed out of the darkness, "Oh boy, I've sure got you covered with a pop-gun!" and a rival electric torch burst into light. Kerrigan swung his own torch round and let it rest upon a man who was standing, pistol in hand, a dozen paces away.

"Put your hands up," said this gentleman pleasantly, "and keep them up till I say the word."

A swift and expert search revealed that Kerrigan carried, by way of arsenal, no firearms, but two lengths of gas-pipe and a pair of knuckle-dusters. The man with the pistol annexed these.

"Now," he said, lighting a small but powerful oil-lantern, "let's have all the news."

Kerrigan looked at him with interest. He was a tough-looking citizen with a very thick, short neck and square shoulders and ugly, knobbly hands. He was only redeemed from downright ugliness by a cheerful gleam in his pale blue eyes. He looked a rascal, but a rascal with a sense of humour.

"The chief bit of news," said Kerrigan, "is that we're locked in."

"You don't say!" replied the thug casually, and Kerrigan knew at once that one problem was solved. There was an alternative exit to the cellar, or the man would have displayed more emotion at finding himself a prisoner.

"And what are you doing down here, boy?" went on the other.

"Looking for mice," replied Kerrigan, and the American laughed.

"Well, you've sure caught more than you expected! Still I'm glad you've come, boy. I was getting mighty lonesome down here. Don't get fresh, though! I'd hate to have to load you up with lead. I'd get lonesome again if I had to bump you off."

"That's all right," replied Peter heartily. "I know the business end of a gun when I see one. I'm not one of your storm-troops. Well, and what's it all about?"

The American pulled out a chair from the heap of old furniture in the corner and sat down comfortably, and crossed his legs and put the pistol on his knee.

"Oh, it's just a spot of business," he observed. "My boss is after some game or other and I'm waiting for orders. That's all."

"What is the game?"

The gunman yawned.

"Oh boy, I don't know, and if I did, I don't think I would run round shouting the good tidings to perfect strangers."

"Do you mind if I sit down, too?" asked Kerrigan, and without waiting for an answer he pulled out another chair and sat down. His mind was racing furiously. He was in a fix and at the moment he could see no way out. It was getting on for eleven o'clock and things would soon be starting to move aloft. It would be the height of folly to attempt any rash *coup de temps* against this square-headed tough. But the square-headed tough solved the problem himself. He was a man who could shoot like a machine, face other people's bullets, stand loyally by his boss through thick and thin, run incredible risks unflinchingly, but he could not stand being bored. For over an hour he had been sitting alone in a dark, damp cellar, and there was every prospect of having to sit there for several hours more. It was an intolerable situation.

"Say!" he exclaimed hoarsely and suddenly, "do you play the poker-game at all, mister?" and he produced a pack of cards from his pocket. Kerrigan tried very hard not to let a flash of elation come into his eyes; he dropped his eyelids, and said:

"I used to play a bit. I haven't played lately very much."

"Care for a game?" asked the other with elaborate carelessness.

"I don't mind."

"No tricks now. Or you'll never open another jackpot on this side of hell. Do you understand?"

"Of course I do. I'm not fool enough to play around with that gun."

"Good," said the thug. "Fetch out one of those tables."

When the table was set, the American laid the pistol down beside his right hand and began to deal. In the middle of the deal he stopped and remarked, "I'm a sportsman, see? I could take all your wad of dollars without having to play for them, see? But I'm a sportsman, and I like a game. Now, ante up, and don't get fresh."

For four or five hands they played in silence—Kerrigan winning two or three small pots and his opponent a couple of slightly larger ones. Then Kerrigan held three tens and defeated three fives, and the American paid over four pounds and frowned. A few minutes later Kerrigan defeated a straight with a flush, and the American paid over eleven pounds and scowled. Kerrigan judged that the time had come for opening his campaign. It was his deal, and he dealt himself three sevens and his opponent a pair of kings. He drew two pairs to fill his full-house and gave his opponent a pair of aces and a king. A moment or two later the highly gratified American was raking in seventeen pounds odd. From then onwards the latter won steadily. Kerrigan's dealing was skilful, and his play was suitably adjusted to the hands which he allotted to his opponent and himself. After a quarter of an hour he decided that the moment had come for the decisive stroke. He would have liked to have left it longer, but he simply did not dare. Even now it might be too late. Anything might be happening upstairs. Battle, Murder, and Sudden Death might be in full swing, and, worse still, his quarter share in a million pounds sterling might be vanishing.

"Have you got any more dough?" inquired the jubilantly triumphant American. "I've got a whole packet of these pounds of yours," and he crumpled up the pile of notes in front of him into a ball.

"I've got a few more," said Kerrigan, dealing himself four tens and his opponent four nines, and recapturing sixty-five pounds. The jubilation faded abruptly and the scowl darkened as Kerrigan remarked sneeringly, "You damned Yanks think you know a thing or two about poker, eh? It's like robbing blind puppies."

"You shut your mouth, blast you!" said the bandit furiously, laying his hand on his gun.

"Go on, shoot!" replied Kerrigan. "You can get money that way. You'll never get it by poker."

The other dealt sulkily and a small pot went to Kerrigan. The supreme moment had arrived. Kerrigan dealt himself the two, three, four, and five of hearts, and drew the six of hearts to complete his straight flush. He dealt the American the seven, eight, nine, ten, and knave of spades. The bidding stopped at two hundred and ten pounds when Kerrigan, leaning back in his chair, obviously well out of reach of the pistol, said with a jeering little laugh:

"I'm going to see you, and I'm going to collect your money, Mr Damned Yank. There you are: Two of hearts, three of hearts, four of hearts, five of hearts, six of hearts! Run away back to Yankland, boy, and learn ludo.

The American looked at the cards, and then a shattering laugh echoed round the cellar, as he put his cards down, one by one as Kerrigan had done, saying between laughs:

"Seven of spades, eight of spades, nine of spades, ten of spades, jack of spades," and finishing up with another roar.

Kerrigan lay a little farther back in his chair, stretched his legs out under the table, and kicked the American a terrific blow on the right elbow. Then he sprang up, knocking the table over as he did so, and hit him accurately upon the point of the jaw. The bandit went over backwards, and Kerrigan, ignoring the Queensberry rules, public-school traditions, and the British sense of fair-play and sportsmanship, instead of waiting for the prostrate adversary to rise, kicked him sharply on the jaw again. Complete silence fell upon the cellar, broken only by a gentle laugh as Kerrigan stooped and picked up the pistol.

He then resumed possession of his own humbler armament of lead-piping and knuckle-dusters, carefully pocketed all the pound notes, and then made a rapid survey of the cellar. He soon found what he was looking for—a length of rope—and it only took him a moment or two to tie up his recent poker adversary into a condition resembling an ancient Egyptian mummy. Kerrigan had once served for a few months as a sailor, and he was good at knots. Then, after rolling the mummy into a corner out of the way, he took the lantern and went to look for the exit which he knew must exist. Its discovery was an easy matter, for the bandit had left the door open. It was a low door, whitewashed to match the cellar walls, and it fitted with extraordinary smoothness and exactitude into its place, so that when it was shut it was impossible to distinguish between it and the surrounding wall. It was heavily backed with bricks, presumably to prevent its being discovered by a betraying echo, and it swung on massive iron hinges, which, he noticed, had been recently oiled.

Kerrigan went through it, lantern in one hand and gun in the other, and down a narrow passage which ended in another door leading into a long-disused, half-subterranean washhouse. Three stone steps led from the washhouse into the garden, and a yard or two from the top of the steps a large motor-bicycle and side-car was standing under the shelter of a spreading rhododendron.

Kerrigan was much too cautious a campaigner to put down his lantern and his gun in order to rub his hands with delight, but that was what he felt like doing. From being locked helpless in a dark cellar, he had already so transformed the situation that he was now fully armed, and had placed himself astride of the line of retreat of one of his opponents. It was definitely a good beginning. The next point to be decided was whether or not to put the motor-bicycle out of action. It would certainly prevent the escape of somebody, presumably the Duke, and if that somebody had got hold of the Treasure, or even of the second clue only, it would be a matter of the most vital importance to prevent their escape. On the other hand, suppose that the owner of the motor-bicycle had failed to get hold of what he was after, and was flying for his life, it would be decidedly unpleasant to compel him to stay at the Manor and fight his way to safety on foot. The Duke at bay, with nothing to lose by displaying the accuracy of his marksmanship, would be a tough proposition. Kerrigan decided to compromise by letting almost all the petrol out of the tank. It was nearly full, and he drained away all except a quarter of an inch into a large tin bath which he found in the cobwebby washhouse. Then he extinguished the lantern and proceeded on hands and knees cautiously round the house. There were two main dangers which he had to contend with—the professional skill of the Duke, and the amateur-ish clumsiness of Streatfield and his melodramatic Colombian. Probably, he reflected, Tarzan was at that very moment creeping about in the garden on his tummy with a knife in his teeth. During a youth spent in the jungles of Colombia he must have become an expert in the art of stealthy night-rambling. He might be lurking in every shadow or following him with murderous and noiseless footsteps. Kerrigan could not prevent himself from looking over his shoulder. He could have sworn he saw something move near that big beech tree. There it was again—and again. Kerrigan held his breath and lay as flat as he could. There was a long silence. An owl hooted very loudly from a plane tree almost overhead, and Kerrigan, his eyes fixed on the shadows at the foot of the beech, wondered if the Colombian had taken to tree-climbing.

Then the thing moved again, quite definitely this time, and an elderly rabbit came trotting slowly out on to the centre of the lawn and sat down to admire the view.

"Stout fellow!" thought Kerrigan with a sigh of relief. "So long as you sit there and don't get the wind up, it means that my rear is all safe. Avanti, Savoi-ardi," and he crept forward again towards the back of the house. A few yards farther on he stopped again. Light footsteps were coming very quickly up a gravel path in front of him, and then he saw for a brief moment the silhouette of what looked like either a woman or a boy muffled up in a long overcoat hurrying past, holding what looked extremely like a rifle or a shot-gun. The silhouette vanished against a background of dark shrubs, and the next moment there was the sound of a door being cautiously opened and shut. Kerrigan backed under the protection of a weeping willow to consider this new development. The gun might not have been a gun at all; that was one alternative. It might have been the boot-boy returning from a little nocturnal fishing expedition. Or it might have been a housemaid who had been on her evening out, and had taken a stick to reassure herself against the possibility of encountering tramps or drunks. Or it might have been the Duke himself. He was said to be a smallish man. On the other hand that was a little unlikely, because the Duke would surely not use a rifle or a shotgun. But again it might have been the Duke carrying something else—an oxyacetylene burner, for instance, or a rope-ladder, or anyone of a score of implements and contrivances for making away with other people's quarter-shares in hidden treasure. Anyway, whoever it was, he had got in by the back door, and Kerrigan determined to try and do the same. It was easier than he had anticipated. A nervous kitchen-maid in a dressing-gown opened the door on the chain and peered out anxiously.

"I'm very sorry to bother you," said Kerrigan softly. "I'm one of the guests in the house and I'm locked out. I wonder if you would mind letting me in? I don't want to disturb the butler by ringing the front-door bell."

The girl, after a moment's hesitation, undid the chain and let him in.

"You're up late," said Kerrigan pleasantly, as he entered. "Been out?"

"Oh no, sir," stammered the maid.

"Ah! I saw someone come in just in front of me. I wondered who it was."

"No—no one came in, sir. Mr Harding gave us strict orders, sir, that no one was to be let in."

"Mr Harding?"

"The butler, sir."

"But you let me in."

"Oh, you're different, sir. You're a guest, sir. I recognized you as soon as I could make you out in the darkness."

Kerrigan pulled a pound note out of his coat-pocket—one of the many notes that had recently been crumpled in the fist of the now mummified bandit—and handed it to the girl.

"Many thanks for your trouble," he said, "and there's another of these for you if you'll tell me the name of the person who came in just now."

"There wasn't anyone, sir."

"Yes, yes, there was. Carrying a gun. Come, a couple of pounds."

"No, sir. I promised I wouldn't tell, and I'm not going to tell."

"Oh dear, what a bore!" said Kerrigan. "You're the sort of girl that's got a conscience, are you?"

"Yes, sir, and I'm not ashamed of it."

"Quite right, too; quite right. Would fifty pounds be any good towards soothing it?"

But the girl only grew sullen. She obviously did not believe for a moment that she would ever see even a fraction of fifty pounds if she gave the information, and she felt that she was being "put upon." Kerrigan saw that it was useless and he left her, after assuring her that he would not reveal her guilty secret to Mr Harding, the great and omnipotent.

He slipped noiselessly through the green baize door which separates in all well-regulated households the servants' hall from the rest of the house, and paused to listen for sounds of clamour and strife. Everything was quiet.

XV

The Duke Gets In

The first thing that struck Kerrigan was that all the lights were burning in the passages. The place was a perfect blaze. He concluded that Lord Claydon and Ilford had had a glimmer of common sense; darkness would certainly suit the book of the two rival parties of treasure-hunters. The second thing that struck Kerrigan was the fact that if darkness was of great importance to the treasure-hunters, then the main switch of the Manor lights was one of the key-points in the battlefield. Sooner or later one or other of the combatants would come creeping down the passage towards the main switch. The power to plunge the Manor into complete darkness at a given moment might easily turn the scale in favour of the party controlling the switch.

Kerrigan returned through the baize door and went down the three steps to the passage where the switch was situated. There was a door at the far end of the passage which could be locked and bolted, but there were no means of securing the baize door. It was, therefore, impossible to isolate the switch. It was at the mercy of anyone who knew where it was or who happened to stumble upon it. Nor was it a thing that was likely to be easily overlooked, being a large, shiny brass lever, protruding about nine inches from its groove in the wall and labelled "Main Switch" on a brass label screwed into the wall below it. Above it was a formidable array of fuse-boxes, dials, wires, and all that central apparatus of an electric-lighting equipment which so resembles part of the interior of a submarine. There was no possibility of mistaking it. There, beyond all reasonable doubt, was the Main Switch.

Kerrigan cast his eyes round for a solution of his problem and lit upon one at once. On the opposite wall of the passage there was a second switch, smaller and less highly polished than the other, labelled "Fire Alarm." A card was pinned on to the wall below the label, and on it was written, "Pull down to ring firebells and communicate with Bicester Fire Station." With the assistance of a trusty pocket-screwdriver, it took Peter Kerrigan about one minute and a quarter to transpose the two labels, and then, shaking with silent laughter, he went back through the baize door, and into the main lounge hall of the Manor.

There was no one there, and he sat down in a big arm-chair, pulled a sofa in front of him so that he was not visible to anyone coming into the lounge, and waited. He was in a commandingly central position so far as the main part of the house was concerned. The library, of course, was outside his range of seeing or hearing, but that could not be helped. All the other conspirators would be concentrating passionately on the library, and it would be madness to attempt to butt in at this eleventh hour. All tactical points of vantage would have been snapped up ages ago, like the front row of the pit or the unreserved seats at Wimbledon. He wondered whether they had lined up in a queue for them. The Colombian was probably sitting up in the gallery armed with a blow-pipe, while Streatfield lurked about in the shadows below with a perfect battery of pistols. Kerrigan tried for the fiftieth time to picture what was likely to happen, and for the fiftieth time gave it up. He had never in his life been involved in an affair of such obscurity and difficulty and uncertainty. To be competing with two rival gangs was nothing new; but it was a novelty not to have the faintest idea what he was competing for.

The sound of footsteps from the direction of the billiard-room interrupted his meditations, and a moment later, by peering round his arm-chair, he was able to see the powerful figure of Sir George Ilford striding slowly into the hall, shooting quick glances right and left as he came. He went to the front door, tried the locks and bolts, and then tested all the windows. When he came over to Kerrigan's corner, he started on seeing that young gentleman asleep on a sofa, hair tousled, face red, breathing loud.

"Here!" exclaimed Ilford, "what are you doing here? Wake up!" and he shook him roughly.

Kerrigan opened his eyes and smiled benevolently. "Dear old egg," he murmured dreamily, "why is it that I associate you with the suburbs of London?" and he closed his eyes again.

"You're as drunk as an owl!" said Ilford angrily, shaking him again.

"Your name is Wandsworth," replied Kerrigan, getting up slowly, running his hands through his hair, blinking foolishly, and smiling. "Come on, Wandsworth, action! Action! that's the cry. You lead and I follow. Or shall I follow and you lead? Whichever you like; it's all one to me. But if you don't mind I'll just have a nap first. Forty winks save one, as the Bible says. Night-night, Tooting, old chap," and he lay down again on the sofa.

With an exclamation of disgust, Ilford tested the window behind the sofa and then marched to the staircase. As he reached the foot of it, Lord Claydon appeared at the top.

"All right, George?"

"Yes. All right. Everything's as right as a trivet."

"Same here. I thought I heard voices."

"It's only that insurance tout. He's dead drunk on a sofa over there. That's all."

"What do you think we ought to do with him?"

"Oh, leave him," said Ilford impatiently. "It doesn't matter what happens to him.

"Good-night, Uncle Harry," said a girl's voice from one of the first-floor corridors; "it's high time you were in bed."

"Is that you, Rosemary? Good-night."

Kerrigan could see the girl join Lord Claydon and lean over the banisters. She was wearing a flimsy silk dressing-gown and blue pyjamas and elegant, high-heeled bedroom slippers.

"Everyone's gone to bed, I suppose," she remarked, "except you two gay old night-birds?"

"Almost everyone," said Ilford with a dry laugh. "Shall I switch the lights out?" asked Rosemary. "No, my dear," replied Lord Claydon with a touch of nervousness in his manner, "I'll do all that." She craned her neck over and remarked:

"Don't forget the lights in the billiard-room. They seem to be in full swing. And the passage leading to the dining-room."

"All right, all right!" said Lord Claydon testily. "You needn't worry about the lights."

"I'm only trying to save you expense," replied the girl blandly. "I hate to see such a waste."

There was a pause. It looked as if a deadlock had set in. Neither of them made a move.

"Well, bedtime!" said Lord Claydon feebly, but nothing happened until Ilford went slowly up the stairs, nodded to Claydon and the girl, and vanished. "Time you were in bed, Rosemary," said Lord Claydon.

"Oh, I'm not going to bed for ages yet," she replied, "I'm not a bit sleepy. I think I'll go down and look at the *Sketch* for a bit."

"Oh, but I say—" began her guardian, but she tripped past him and went nimbly downstairs and ensconced herself with a sheaf of evening and illustrated papers on the very sofa which was screening the somnolent drunkard.

"Good-night, uncle," she cried. "You can leave the lights to me."

Lord Claydon began to come downstairs, paused irresolutely, and then said:

"How long are you likely to be?"

"Oh, about half an hour or so."

"Very well." He hovered about uncertainly and then turned and went along one of the corridors in the direction, not of his own room, but of Ilford's, seeking, presumably, comfort and advice.

Rosemary selected the *Sketch* and the *Tatler*, and threw the other papers on the floor beside her, and deep silence settled upon the main lounge hall of Marsh Manor. It lasted for about ten minutes, and was broken by the characteristically quiet arrival of Mr Tollemache—the mild-looking, world-wide celebrity in the art world and, as alleged, in the blackmailing world as well. His footsteps were almost noiseless and his voice was soft and caressing.

"Still up, Miss Shackleford?" he murmured, moving a chair in front of the sofa and sitting down facing her. "I thought I was the last. I've been almost asleep, I'm sorry to say. What do you think are the chances of finding the Treasure?"

The girl betrayed no sign of surprise at the sudden directness of the question.

"I've no idea," she replied. "Are you also a competitor in the great search?"

"Everyone is naturally interested in the whereabouts of a million pounds, even if it does not belong to oneself. It isn't lost, what a friend gets."

"You mean that you can always borrow from him?"

"I meant rather that one delights in his good fortune."

"Very Christian of you," said the girl dryly.

"And what is your opinion of the nature of the Treasure?" went on the art-collector. "Or, better still, of its whereabouts?"

"I have no idea about either."

"And yet surely a clever girl like you must have solved the puzzle in those samplers?"

Kerrigan almost betrayed himself with an exclamation. Rosemary answered truthfully:

"Oh yes, that was easy. How long did it take you, Mr Tollemache?"

"To tell you the truth, I didn't actually do it myself. A friend of mine did it, and told me about it."

"And are you following up what your friend told you? I mean, are you taking an active interest in the Treasure-hunt, or merely an academic interest?"

"Believing as I do that the Treasure probably consists of pictures by Leonardo or Ver Meer, I am taking both an active and academic interest. And so you've got as far as clue number one, Miss Shackleford? Do you suppose that anyone else in the house has?"

The girl laughed.

"No, frankly, I don't believe that Uncle Harry or Sir George could rise to the pure heights of intellect required for the solution of the problem. I fancy that only your anonymous friend and I have managed it."

"What about that young man with the curly brown hair?"

She laughed again, gaily and light-heartedly.

"Poor Mr Kerrigan!" she replied. "I don't think he's one of the world's heaven-born puzzle solvers. At the present moment he's rather drunk and locked in the cellar."

"What!" said Mr Tollemache sharply.

"I said that dear little Mr Kerrigan is at present rather drunk and locked in the cellar. Is there anything worrying you, Mr Tollemache?"

"Nothing whatever," he answered, with all his habitual mild blandness.

Kerrigan was puzzled. The little blackmailing art-dealer had unquestionably been put out at the mention of the cellar. His tone of voice and the fact that the girl had asked him whether anything was worrying him, was sufficient proof of that. Was it possible that the unfortunate poker-playing thug was a friend, not of the Duke, but of Mr Tollemache? That was perfectly possible. In which case the blackmailer was a more formidable factor than he had allowed for. He had regarded him hitherto as a man playing a lone hand, and playing it quietly and without violence. But if the thug below-stairs was in his troupe, then he would have to be added to the already sufficiently numerous throng of potential gunmen. Another question that was less important, although undeniably interesting, was how he had hit upon the solution of the samplers? Of course he might be bluffing; he might know nothing whatsoever about the solution. That was a point which would probably be settled later.

Mr Tollemache continued in his soft, ingratiating voice:

"I don't believe you understand me one little bit, my dear young lady. I don't think you like me very much, and I'm sure you don't trust me."

"I see no reason," was the cool reply, "why I should either trust or distrust you. I don't know you very well, after all."

"Perhaps you will allow me to explain," he went on, "exactly what my position is. I have three duties." His explanation of his position and his triple obligations was rudely interrupted by the arrival, headlong and breathless, of one of the footmen from the upper parts of the house. He was dressed in shirt, socks, and trousers and he was extremely agitated and excited, exclaiming repeatedly, "My lord, my lord, my lord!" In the twinkling of an eye, Lord Claydon, Ilford, the butler, and Lady Caroline (in a fearful and wonderful dressing-gown of purple satin, and a lace cap), appeared on the first floor. The first three ran downstairs; Lady Caroline stayed above.

"My lord, my lord!" reiterated the footman. "A window at the end of the wing. I saw you and Harding shut it, my lord, and bolt the shutters—and now it's open, wide open!"

"Good God!" cried Ilford, racing up the stairs three steps at a time. "Which way? Which way?" He came back in a moment or two. "Yes," he said briefly. "It's open, and there's a rope-ladder hanging from the sill."

There was silence for a moment, and then Lord Claydon said heavily:

"That means the Duke is inside the house."

XVI

Kerrigan "Contra Mundum"

"Personally," said Mr Tollemache quietly after a moment, "I am rather sceptical about the existence of that gentleman. I think you will find, my dear Claydon, that one of your admirable staff of domestics is conducting a harmless little flirtation in your conveniently adjacent, and if I may say so, conveniently sequestered woods."

"Where's Gerald and his servant fellow?" cried Lord Claydon, paying no attention to him. "Why didn't they hear the alarm?"

Lady Pamela, who had joined Lady Caroline on the first floor, answered both questions with a cold off-handedness.

"They're patrolling the house. Just because they aren't in hysterics in the lounge it doesn't mean that they didn't hear the alarm."

Lord Claydon was immensely relieved.

"Of course," he exclaimed. "I'd forgotten that they are on guard. Nothing can happen while they're on guard. Let's all go back to bed. Come on, George. Rosemary, Tollemache!"

He led the way upstairs. Only the agitated footman followed him. Sir George Ilford said abruptly: "Rosemary, where exactly is Gerald?"

"I don't know."

"He must be told about this business at once."

"How are you going to tell him if you can't find him?"

This baffled Sir George, and he stared helplessly round. Rosemary went across and laid a hand on his arm.

"Look here, George," she said. "Gerald has got the whole thing in hand. Why worry? He and Esteban are a match for about half a dozen men at any time. And here they've got the advantage of knowing the ground and being ready beforehand. You can leave everything to them. Run away to bed. Good-night. Good-night, Mr Tollemache."

Ilford looked at her doubtfully and said:

"I suppose you know more about Gerald's plans than I do."

"Of course she does," interrupted Lady Pamela. "And so do I. Why can't you leave well alone?"

"I can't see where the 'well' comes in, if that fellow has got into the house through that open window."

"Can't you understand that 'that fellow' as you call him, isn't expecting to meet people like Gerald and Esteban, whereas they are expecting to meet him?"

"Very well," said Ilford. "If you're so cocksure, you can go ahead with it. I'm not going to butt in, because I haven't got a gun, and I doubt if I would if I had."

He went upstairs again to his room. Lady Pamela leaned on the balustrade. Lady Caroline had already taken herself and her purple dressing-gown off.

"Good-night, Mr Tollemache," said Rosemary, holding out her hand.

"I have, as I was saying," said Mr Tollemache, sitting down, "three duties. One to myself, which impels me to make as much money and collect as many pictures as I can; secondly, towards Lord Claydon, who did me a very good turn years ago when I was very nearly down and out; and thirdly, towards Art. Now, as a general rule, my dear young lady, I am bound to confess that I look after my own interests first. It is only natural. But here is a case in which my own interests are diametrically opposed to those of Lord Claydon and of Art. For if this famous Treasure is discovered, Lord Claydon will not need to sell me his collection of Old Masters, and I shall lose the chance of a lifetime. So the discovery of the Treasure will help Lord Claydon but not me. Furthermore, if the Treasure proves to be lost Leonardos or Ver Meers, the immortal cause of Art will be vastly benefited. It is two to one, dear young lady, and I surrender. I want to help you to find the Treasure. I am on your side!" Kerrigan smiled broadly.

"You old liar!" he said to himself. Rosemary replied at once:

"Thank you very much. I know we are all very grateful to you, Mr Tollemache. You really want to help?"

"I do indeed."

"And so you can. By going off to bed now." Mr Tollemache lowered his voice to a whisper.

"I can help you in another way as well. Can you get hold of that queer-looking Spaniard?" "Esteban?"

"Yes. Get hold of him and tell him to watch George Ilford's window."

Rosemary lowered her voice: "Why?"

"Because Ilford knows where the Treasure is. And there's no one here who can tackle him except Esteban."

"That's true," she murmured. "But are you sure about Ilford?"

"I heard him say to Lord Claydon this evening—just a half-sentence—a word or two—but it was enough. 'Take it to Christie's tomorrow,' was what I heard. Isn't that enough? There's nothing else in the house that he could take to be sold at Christie's. I've got an option on all the valuable stuff. Don't you think that that's conclusive?"

Rosemary looked up at Lady Pamela who had been listening intently from the first floor.

"What about it, Pam?" she said.

"I don't trust George Ilford a foot," replied that lady.

"Shall we warn Gerald?"

"Wouldn't do any harm."

"It isn't Gerald you ought to warn," interposed Mr Tollemache. "It's his servant. Ilford's a man of enormous strength. It will need the servant to tackle him."

"Shall I go and tell him, Rosemary?"

"I think so, Pam. It won't do any harm."

"All right. By the way, where's the insurance tout?"

"Drunk in the cellar."

"Good." Lady Pamela ran off down the passage. "And now, Mr Tollemache, your second piece of assistance," said Rosemary coaxingly. "Run along to bed, and leave everything to us."

"You're sure there's nothing more I can do? I am no fighting man, but I have a certain amount of low cunning which is at your disposal." He laughed a gentle, throaty laugh. "How would it be if you retired for the night and left the field to me instead?"

Rosemary laughed also.

"Nothing doing, Mr Tollemache, I'm afraid. We're in earnest, you know."

"Ah! But so am I. What's that?" he added sharply.

Kerrigan could not see what it was, but Rosemary's next words enlightened him.

"It's only Esteban, on all fours, changing ground." Kerrigan was full of admiration for the girl's light-hearted fearlessness. She might be taking part in a game of hide-and-seek for all the fuss she made, instead of being involved in a game of manœuvre and counter-manœuvre with cut-throats and murderers, for a colossal stake.

"Ah!" said Mr Tollemache. "In that case, I fancy the game is due to begin."

There was a subtle change in his voice. It seemed fresher and younger. Rosemary apparently noticed nothing different about it, for she replied with her usual, off-hand lightness:

"Oh, I thought it had begun ages ago."

"My game is only beginning now," replied Mr Tollemache. "Do you see this neat little bottle, my dear young lady? It contains vitriol."

There was a pause, and then he continued:

"I have found in a long course of experience that it is no earthly use threatening high-spirited young ladies with pistols. They just sneer at them. But vitriol is different. I never yet met a young lady, however spirited, who sneered at vitriol. It does leave such horrid marks."

Kerrigan could hear the girl's breath coming quickly, but she spoke with complete composure when she said: "And which side are you on now, Mr Tollemache?"

"On my own, now that Master Esteban has been cleared out of his room, thanks to you, dear young lady. And now perhaps you will kindly step this way. I think you might as well join your drunken young friend in the cellar. It will keep you out of mischief. No tricks now, or your exquisite appearance will become a good deal less exquisite in the immediate future."

Rosemary did exactly what Kerrigan would have done in the same circumstances. She neither swore nor protested nor implored. She went in front of Mr Tollemache towards the cellar without a word.

"Good girl!" murmured the art-valuer with a chuckle. "Good, obedient girl!"

Kerrigan peeped round the sofa and watched them disappear round the corner of the passage. Tollemache's new and militant activity introduced an additional factor of some slight importance. It meant an extra amount of vigilance. Another new factor was Tollemache's anxiety to get Esteban away from his room. Kerrigan was just wondering what that meant when he got a nasty shock. His eyes happened to light upon an evening paper which was lying among the heap that Rosemary had deposited on the floor beside the sofa, and he read, mechanically, a paragraph in the stop-press news which ran as follows:

"CLAPHAM COMMON MURDER.

"The body of the man found buried on Clapham Common this morning has been identified as that of a Mr William Morganson Tollemache, a well-known art-dealer, valuer, and private collector."

He read it twice before the full implication of it sprang up and hit him between the eyes, and then a whole lot of things explained themselves in a flash which had been inexplicable before. The chief and main and overwhelming implication was that the gentleman who had been masquerading at Marsh Manor for weeks and weeks as Mr Tollemache, who was at that moment strolling towards the cellar-door with Miss Shackleford, vitriol bottle in hand, was the Duke himself. The position was now enormously complicated. It was not simply that the famous killer was in the very midst of the defences; that was what Kerrigan had reckoned would happen. He was ready for that emergency. But the famous killer was not a stranger fighting upon strange ground. He had been in the place for weeks, planning, spying, plotting, calculating, until he knew the place probably better than anyone else; certainly far better than Kerrigan did. It was the latter now who was fighting on strange ground against an adversary who knew every inch of it. Nor was that all.

Kerrigan during the last few days had kept Tollemache and the Duke in separate water-tight compartments. Such-and-such a thing had been known to one and not to the other and *vice versa*, and plans of action, calculations of possibilities and estimates of probabilities had been based upon this separation into compartments. But now that the two personalities had suddenly been rolled into one, everything was changed with painful abruptness, and Kerrigan had precious little time in which to re-orientate his ideas.

The first and most pressing eventuality to be guarded against was that the Duke might take advantage of his visit to the cellar to have a word with the mummified bandit who was now certain to be one of his colleagues. If he did, he would very quickly realise that Kerrigan was at large in the house, was a formidable opponent, and armed with the bandit's pistol. If, on the other hand, he did not speak to his colleague but simply pushed the girl in, then it would not be long before she found her way out into the washhouse and thence into the garden.

Another possibility that might materialise at any moment—indeed, Kerrigan was rather surprised that it had not done so already—was the arrival of the police. It would not take long for Fleming to connect the body on Clapham Common with the gentleman who had been staying at Marsh Manor. Kerrigan could not help wishing that Fleming would waste as little time as possible in putting in an appearance. In the meantime, there was nothing to be done but to wait and watch. In less than a minute Mr Tollemache came back slowly, with his eyes fixed on the ground. Kerrigan shifted the pistol in his coat pocket to a more convenient angle and waited. He did not dare to look round the corner of the sofa again, but he could hear the other man's breathing. A moment later he heard the breathing recede, and then a creak on the stair. He flashed a quick look round the sofa, saw Mr Tollemache go slowly upstairs, and turn down the corridor which led to the region of Esteban's room and the window which had been opened and rope-laddered.

Kerrigan slipped off his shoes and ran noiselessly after him. At the corner of the passage he lay down and peered round an inch or two from the floor.

The Duke had opened the window again and was picking up the rope-ladder, which had been left on the floor beside the window, and was fixing it again to the window-sill. Then he pulled out a key, unlocked the door of Esteban's room and went in, locking it behind him.

Kerrigan tiptoed down the passage and listened at the keyhole. There was a cracking sound, as if someone was snapping thin bits of wood across his knee, several times repeated. Then there was a pause and the sound of a heavy bit of furniture being moved. The Duke was obviously hot on the trail. He knew where to look and he was looking. At any moment he might find the Treasure or the second clue, and then he would come out again and the shooting would begin.

Kerrigan decided that face-to-face shooting in a corridor would be no joke, and that an ambush would give him a better chance. He looked round hastily. There was no possibility of ambushing even a mouse in the corridor, which was lamentably deficient in alcoves, dark corners, or protective curves. A brain-wave struck him. The obvious place was in the darkness at the foot of the rope-ladder. It would be a perfect place of concealment, and the Duke, in the comparative elation at having got out of the house, might be more off his guard and easier to surprise. Kerrigan darted across to the window and was just throwing his leg over the sill when he saw the squat, frog-like figure of Esteban coming up the ladder a yard or two below him. The figure of Rosemary Shackleford was faintly discernible on the ground at the foot. But Peter Kerrigan was less concerned with her figure at that moment than with the long knife which Esteban was carrying in his mouth.

He withdrew his head with lightning celerity, and darted down the passage again. Just as he rounded the corner he heard the first attempt of Esteban upon the handle of his bedroom door.

Assuming that the Colombian knife-expert could be trusted to perform the traditional role of the bull-dog and remain on guard at the bedroom door, Kerrigan was safe to dash round the outside of the house and cut off the Duke's retreat via the bedroom window. That the Duke had a retreat via the bedroom window, Kerrigan did not doubt for an instant. Probably he had half a dozen different lines of retreat, but the obvious thing was to cover the bedroom window. Kerrigan had to chance the Colombian's movements, and he rushed downstairs. At the foot of the stairs he was seized with a happy inspiration, and he ran up again and, halting at the corner so that he was invisible from the end of the passage, whispered with a penetrating hoarseness in his best South American Spanish, "Guard that door, Esteban. Whatever you do, guard that door!"

"That ought to fix Tarzan," he thought, as the answering whisper of "*Sí, señor, sí señor,*" came down the passage, and he was free to concentrate upon getting out.

To get out of the house quickly was not so easy a task as it sounded. Every door and window was bolted and barred, and it was a question of choosing the one which would most readily yield to Peter's bunch of skeleton keys and twisted wires. He decided on the back door, and dived through the green baize and started to work. It took him about four minutes to get out, longer than he had anticipated, but there were two separate locks to be negotiated.

Once outside he vanished into a shrubbery and worked his way along the house until he was opposite the room of the first floor which he judged to be Esteban's. There was a light burning in it; occasionally a shadow appeared on the wall; and the window was open. The Duke was evidently still at work.

"What a magnificently cool fellow!" thought Kerrigan enviously. "Wanted for murder a dozen times over; knows that he's surrounded by chaps after him; must hear old Mowgli scrabbling at the door, and yet he works away, cool as bedamned, as if he owned the earth. Wish I was like that!"

He settled down on hands and knees behind a row of sweet-peas in a flower-bed, and glanced along the house towards the tall outline of the library. Presumably Streatfield was wasting his time on guard there, or doing something equally futile and footling. Then he suddenly remembered the figure of Rosemary Shackleford on the grass at the foot of the rope-ladder. Damn it! what a fool he had been not to lock the door of the washhouse. But then he couldn't have known at the time how important it would be not to let that infernal girl realise the whole situation. She knew as much as anyone now—except, perhaps, that Tollemache was the Duke, and she would probably guess that with some blasted feminine intuition. She hadn't wasted a moment in fetching up her troops once she got out of the cellar; she was like Napoleon—put her fingers on the hub of the thing at once and got hold of Tarzan and slung him into the fray to blockade the bedroom door. Her next move—Peter Kerrigan jumped as if he had been stung—her next move, of course, would be to get hold of Streatfield and sling him into the fray to blockade the bedroom window. He would be here at any minute with his arsenal of firearms, and a border of sweet-peas, however decorative, cannot by any stretch of the imagination be called bullet-proof.

His guess was correct. A moment or two later there was a crackling of pine-needles away to his left, followed by a stealthy rustling, and then Streatfield's crouching figure appeared a few yards away, taking post behind a tree.

"The Duke," thought Kerrigan, "is in rather a tight place."

The tightness of his place lay, of course, in his ignorance of Rosemary's easy exit from the cellar, and in the consequent swift mobilisation of her allies. On the other hand, he was a gentleman of undeniable quickness and resource. He had about an even chance, thought Kerrigan.

The next instant the light went out in Esteban's room. The Duke had found what he was looking for. The Grand Retreat was about to begin. It began in complete silence. There was not a sound for perhaps five minutes. It was impossible to see from the ground anything that was happening inside that darkened room and Kerrigan concentrated his watchfulness upon a patch of light below the dark window that was cast by illuminations elsewhere in the house. Anyone sliding down a ladder, or letting down a ladder to slide down, would be bound to attract attention in this zone of reflected light upon the wall.

Suddenly a heavy mass, looking very like the body of a man, fell across the zone of light to the ground, and Streatfield straightened himself and opened fire. The dark mass lay very still in the shadow at the foot of the wall. A terrific banging and thumping from inside the house seemed to indicate that Esteban had launched his assault major upon the bedroom door.

A minute more and the whole house would be up and abroad. Another heavy mass fell from the darkened window, and again Streatfield fired at it as it reached the ground, and again it lay very still at the bottom of the wall.

Kerrigan shot a sidelong look at Streatfield and saw that he was feverishly putting a new clip of cartridges into his automatic; he was far too excited to be on the alert for anything except the targets which had descended or were likely to descend from that window. Kerrigan got up as silently as he could and moved away from him. He had no desire to be anywhere near the man who was advertising himself as the possessor of firearms and an inclination to use them. It was a good move, for, hardly had he slipped away a dozen yards when there was a terrific flash and an ear-splitting explosion, about ten feet in front of Streatfield's tree. The Duke's bomb-throwing practice was good for direction, but not quite good enough for strength. The deafening clap of the explosion was followed by a simultaneous burst of excitement and indignation from every bird within a mile of the Manor, the cawing of rooks vastly predominating as they rose and wheeled and flapped in their hundreds above the woods.

But Kerrigan did not object to the noise nor, after he had made certain that he was not hit, to the bits of flying metal which hurtled over his head in all directions. It was the three or four seconds of absolute darkness after the flash that he objected to. For it was obviously in those three or four seconds that the American gunman was going to make the first move of his retreat. The only thing to do, therefore, was to advance at once towards the wall below the window and trust to the blinding darkness evaporating before he reached it. Pistol in hand, therefore, and crouching as low as possible, he made straight for the house, tripped over a strand of wire that was assisting some plant or other to reach its full development, and fell flat on his face. He got up in time to see a dark figure running with incredible agility round the house in the direction of the hidden motor-bicycle.

"That'll worry him," thought Peter, as he jumped to his feet. "He'll be expecting his pal to have got it started for him."

The next moment he flung himself down again, for a bullet from behind had taken off the tip of his left ear. The bomb had not accounted for Streatfield, apparently. This view was confirmed by the sound of that gentleman's voice roaring out, "Esteban, Esteban, *venga, venga!*"

A crash and a splintering of woodwork from the bedroom above was evidence of the Colombian's success at last in breaking down the door; the lights were switched on, and the next moment the Colombian jumped out of the window on to the pile at the foot of the wall, which was now revealed to be mattresses and pillows.

"Here he is, here he is!" shouted Streatfield, forgetting his Spanish in the excitement of the moment, and blazing away into the trees above Kerrigan's prostrate body.

"Tut-tut!" thought that individual, as the bullets crashed into the undergrowth or glanced off tree-trunks, "this is a trifle warm. Blast the fellow!" He whipped out of his pocket the electric torch with the long, expandable arm which he had found in the library on the occasion of Rubin's murder, extended the arm to its maximum length into the flower-beds, switched it on, jumped up, and ran for his life towards a clump of trees. Streatfield extinguished the light in four seconds, and Peter reached the trees in three and a half. But the Colombian had not seen the electric light and he had seen the flying figure, and he set off in pursuit with huge, bounding strides like a gorilla. He seemed to be a man who despised new-fangled weapons such as gunpowder and Colt revolvers, for in his hand he carried his favourite long, shiny knife.

Kerrigan, who had halted for a moment under cover of a massive beech tree to take stock of the situation, saw him coming, a fearsome, primeval spectacle. But the only tactical problem which his dervish-like onslaught presented, was how to shoot him without drawing Streatfield's fire again. At all costs he must keep the beech tree between himself and where he imagined Streatfield to be. Fortunately, the oncoming gorilla saw him and swerved a little in order to get at him round the tree trunk, so that Kerrigan did not have to move. He waited till the man was a dozen yards away and aimed at his great, barrel-like chest, then changed his mind and decided only to bring him down with a shot in the leg. After all, he did not want to do the poor faithful devil a serious injury, let alone be run in before an English jury on a homicide charge. He pulled the trigger and the pistol jammed.

"That comes of trusting cheap American goods," he said aloud, as he flung the pistol at the Colombian. It hit him fair and square upon the top of the head and bounced off as if it had been a ping-pong ball. Esteban shook his head as a man shakes off a troublesome mosquito and did not slacken speed. Only he lifted his shoulders a little so that he could see his quarry more clearly. Esteban apparently mingled a faint glimmer of common sense with his berserker folly.

There were two courses open to Kerrigan. He could either attempt to draw one of his two useful little pieces of gas-piping and join in a hand-to-hand rough-and-tumble with the Colombian, trusting to be able to finish him off in a second or two and get away before the arrival, pistol in hand, of Streatfield, or else he could turn and make a bolt for it. It took him the barest fraction of a second to make up his mind, and then he turned and bolted in the direction the Duke had gone.

There were several advantages in taking this direction. Firstly, it kept the beech tree for a second or two longer between himself and Streatfield's line of advance; secondly, it made a clash between his two sets of opponents a distinct possibility; and thirdly, it kept him upon the main objective, the recovery of whatever it was that the Duke had removed from Esteban's bedroom. The main disadvantage was that it placed him, practically unarmed, between two heavily-armed and hostile forces.

The race was conducted at a whirlwind speed as far as the corner of the house, with Kerrigan just maintaining his lead. On the other side of the corner he dived down between two yew hedges that led away from the direction of the washhouse, and as there was a choice of three paths, and the hedges cast a deep shadow across all of them, he gained perhaps one second, or eight or nine yards, on the pursuer who hesitated before choosing the right path. Another second was gained in the rose garden, and it was with a lead of about twenty-five yards that he raced back and made a detour for the washhouse. He had heard the sound of a motor-bicycle suddenly spring into life from that direction, and he realised that it was a case of now or never. He had not the faintest idea of what he was going to do when he reached the motor-bicycle, beyond a vague, general strategic notion that his one chance now lay in embroiling the Duke and the Streatfield-Esteban combination.

By this time windows were open, maids were screaming, lights were blazing, Ilford's voice could be heard roaring something in the distance, and Kerrigan, as he braced himself for a final sprint across a now brightly-illuminated lawn, could see at least one female figure hanging out of a first-floor window, gesticulating wildly and apparently screaming. He could also see on his left front, between himself and the house, and racing along to cut him off, the figure of Streatfield with a pistol in each hand. While Esteban had followed him on the detour into the garden, Streatfield had cut off the corners by hugging the wall of the house. The only consolation in an otherwise extremely unconsoling situation was that Streatfield was running straight towards the hidden but now noisy motor-bicycle. Kerrigan glanced over his shoulder. The human gorilla had just bounded clear of the rose-garden and was on the edge of the lawn. The lights of the house shone bravely upon his gleaming knife.

Again Kerrigan had an awkward choice to make, and he postponed it for a second or two by turning right-handed a little so that he was running almost parallel with the house. This at least would bring Streatfield nearer the motor-bicycle. Kerrigan found time to curse the Duke for being so slow to emerge; but, presumably, he was watching the runners and awaiting developments. The female who was leaning out of the window screamed hoarsely and shrilly at Streatfield as he ran past beneath her, and then suddenly levelled a gun to her shoulder and fired straight at Kerrigan. He ducked and swore and simultaneously heard an infuriated bellow behind him. A pattering sound upon the rose-bushes like rain, told him that the gun had been a shot-gun; and the sight of Esteban, rolling about on the lawn and howling, told him that not all the pellets had been wasted upon inoffensive plants; and the shrill voice screaming, "Out of the way, Peter!" told him that the providential shooter was Lady Caroline.

The same instant the sound of the motor-bicycle stopped, and an American voice shouted angrily: "Heine, where in hell are you? We've got to quit!" Kerrigan skipped nimbly out of the line of fire, and the old lady blazed off another salvo of small shot at the unfortunate Colombian. This time her aim was not so true, and the patter on the rose-bushes only had the effect of galvanising Esteban into activity. With a volley of imprecations he sprang up and hobbled out of sight. Streatfield had also vanished. The scene of action seemed to have been transferred once more into the interior of the house.

So far almost everything had gone as far wrong as it was possible for it to go. Kerrigan had placed himself, armed, across the Duke's line of retreat, only to see the blundering Streatfield drive him off it again; he no longer had a pistol; the whole campaign had shifted on to ground that the American knew from A to Z; while the only item upon the asset side was the partial disablement of the amiable Colombian. And then another important item on the debit side struck him forcibly.

Once the American got into the cellar, he would presumably be able to find time to release his colleague, the poker-playing bandit. A few cuts with a knife — it was a matter of a second or two. Together they would form a real Strong-Arm Squad and would probably abandon guile and strategy and simply shoot themselves out, in good old-fashioned Chicago style. They might just as well be hanged for sheep as lambs—a proverb of which they were probably well aware. The only question was, by which exit would they shoot themselves out?

Lady Caroline was calling urgently to him in a whisper, and Kerrigan ran quickly across to her.

"Here you are," she whispered eagerly, handing down her shot-gun, "and here are some cartridges. It was the best I could do. The farmers round here don't seem to keep rifles or revolvers."

"Well done, Lady C.!" he cried enthusiastically, seizing the gun, stuffing in a couple of cartridges and pocketing the rest. "Keep your door locked, and your head down. See you later!" and he ran stealthily to the entrance of the washhouse and peered in.

The American's movements, as usual, had been astonishingly swift and effective. From the time when he had called out, urging his assistant to disclose his whereabouts, to the moment of Streatfield's arrival outside the washhouse, hardly a couple of seconds could have passed. And yet he had rushed into the washhouse, slammed the door in Streatfield's face, entered the cellar, and released his tied-up friend Heine before the few seconds of Streatfield's natural hesitation outside the door of the washhouse had elapsed. When Kerrigan peered into the washhouse, all he could see was Streatfield kneeling at the side of the door into the narrow passage trying to see what was happening in the cellar. He did not have to wait long. A tempest of explosions and flashes lit up the darkness and Streatfield, apparently unhurt, shrank back very naturally into a corner, while the bullets thudded and ricochetted and bounced on the walls of the washhouse. One hit the ceiling just above Kerrigan's head and brought down a handful of plaster and cement. The appalling clatter stopped as abruptly as it had begun, and the dead silence that followed was only broken by a faint clang which Kerrigan at once recognised as the shutting of the iron door at the top of the cellar stairs. The American contingent had carried their retreat right into the house.

Peter left his observation post at the door of the washhouse and ran towards the back door, but, passing on his way the rope-ladder which was still dangling from the window where the pseudo Mr Tollemache had hung it, he changed his mind, seized it, and went up like a lamplighter. But, unlike Esteban, he went up it with his eyes on the window above him instead of on the ground, and just before he reached the top a thick cudgel came over the window-sill, followed by the glorious mass of hair that crowned Miss Shackleford's head, and a peremptory, "Stop!"

"Stop be damned! " said Kerrigan, hauling up hand over hand.

"You be damned," retorted the girl, aiming a vicious blow at his head which he only just succeeded in dodging. It hit him on the shoulder instead and hurt excessively.

"Tut, tut, tut!" he said in some annoyance, pushing her aside firmly, as she hit him another swinger on the elbow, and jumping down into the corridor. "You are the silliest girl I've ever met in my life. You've got as much sense as a hen!" Then, tucking his shot-gun under his arm, he sprinted down the corridor in the direction of the main staircase, pausing at the end to add over his shoulder, "And, as everyone knows, a hen is all beak," and then he ran down the staircase.

Half-way down he stopped abruptly. Standing on the hearth-rug in the lounge-hall below him was a young man with a pink, chubby face. In his left hand he was holding a grey wig, a grey moustache, and a pair of grey side-whiskers, and in his right a large automatic pistol. He was looking up at Kerrigan with mild interest. The first thing that the latter saw about him was that he was not even out of breath. His hand was as steady as a rock, his movements of hand and eye quiet and deliberate.

"Oh boy!" said the young man, "I don't wish you any harm. Drop your cannon." Kerrigan dropped his shot-gun on to the stairs with a clatter. "You'd much best get back to your insurance touting," went on the Anglo-American, glancing casually up to where a confused murmuring, sobbing, and an occasional wail betokened the alarmed condition of the household. "Strong-arm stuff isn't in your line. Take my advice and you'll keep out of these blood-and-thunder entertainments. You aren't cut out for them, laddie. You aren't, really. Now, that Streatfield fellow, he's different. He's a tough egg and no mistake. Any man who can slug my Heine under the jaw and tie him into knots is a tough egg and I wouldn't waste any more time on him than it takes to pull a trigger. But you're a decent little softie. Run away, boy; run away." He threw a glance, again a casual, negligent glance, at the front door, which was standing ajar.

Kerrigan succeeded in producing a woeful stammer as he said:

"But I don't know where to run to. It's all so dangerous everywhere."

The American smiled, and it was a smile of genuine amusement.

"As you say, boy, it is all so dangerous everywhere." Sir George Ilford's dark head appeared over the landing on the first floor for a moment. The American appeared to be looking straight at Kerrigan, but he jerked his wrist with an incredibly swift upward motion and a shot hit the ceiling above the baronet's head. "I don't want to hurt him either," explained the ex-art-valuer, "just to frighten him."

He had succeeded in his object, for the head withdrew with considerable rapidity. The next moment there was a gentle scrunching of wheels on the gravel outside and then Heine, the poker-playing thug, poked his head in at the front door and observed:

"Got it, chief."

"Where's Streatfield?"

"Didn't see him. In the cellar, I guess."

"Oh! Just wait till I switch off the lights. It'll make it easier for us getting away."

The Duke went across to the baize door with lithe, pantherine steps and disappeared. Kerrigan had taken advantage of this brief conversation to edge down half a dozen steps and, when Heine, fully equipped for motoring in black peaked cap and goggles, swung the door open and came into the hall, he was completely covered from the thug by the door. The Duke had no monopoly of quick, silent moving, and Heine only saw over his shoulder the last few feet of Kerrigan's attack. The knuckle-dusters caught him on the back of the head and he went down like a stone. Peter had just stuffed the body behind a sofa, got into the big black coat and peaked cap and was adjusting the goggles, when the air was rent by a tumult of bells, topped by the deep note of the main fire-alarm bell of the Manor. The next instant there was a tempestuous rush of arms, legs, and hairy face through the door, as Esteban, despite his pelleted leg, hurtled through and flung himself upon the figure in the black oilskins. They went to the ground in a heap and rolled over and over and over, Kerrigan gripping the Colombian's knife-wrist like grim death and the other struggling frantically to get it free. The Colombian was immensely more powerful and heavy than Kerrigan, but the latter's wrists were famous in the underworlds of a good many countries, and the long knife remained out of action until two deafening explosions and a loud click sounded as if they had been let off inside Kerrigan's ear-drums. Esteban gave a sigh and went suddenly limp, and then his head fell back with a thud. Kerrigan paused for a moment to pull the peaked cap down over his eyes and adjust his goggles before he jumped up.

The Duke was looking down at the Colombian. "Have two shots done it?" he asked tranquilly. His iron coolness appeared to be quite unshakable. "I would have given him a third but my clip's finished. Come on, Heine—quick. There's something wrong with these blamed lights."

The two men made for the door, colliding slightly in the entrance, and ran down to the motor-bicycle.

"I'll drive," said the Duke, and Kerrigan sprang into the side-car. As they swung down the avenue a couple of bullets hit the fir trees in front of them and they could see the figure of Streatfield standing outside the washhouse.

The Anglo-American chuckled as the powerful bicycle roared out of the park gates on to the Aylesbury Road. Kerrigan lay back in the side-car and wondered how long it would be before they were stopped by a police patrol. After the murder that evening of John Hone—good Heavens! it seemed a month ago—every road would surely be patrolled, if not picketed and blockaded. There wasn't the faintest chance of getting to Aylesbury without being challenged, let alone London.

But apparently the Duke had no intention of going to Aylesbury, for a short distance down the road he turned off to the right to the little village of Ambrosden, and then again up a cart-track just short of the village. At the end of the track there was a gate, and he halted and switched off the lights.

"Here we are, my boy," he remarked gaily. "Three more minutes, and then good-bye to all this." He vaulted nimbly over the gate, and Kerrigan got out of the side-car and followed him across a field to a large shed. The door was quickly swung back, a light switched on, and an aeroplane revealed.

"Go to it, lad," said the Duke. Heine was clearly the pilot-mechanic. Peter had never piloted an aeroplane in his life and did not propose to begin now. He had no objection to flying as a passenger; but as a pilot, no. The obvious moment had arrived for slugging the Duke a quick one behind the ear, when suddenly the other man seemed to have an inspiration that something was wrong. Whether it was Kerrigan's momentary hesitation before he got to business, or whether it was something unfamiliar about his build, or whether the sudden light revealed a chin less unshaven than Mr Heine's azure jaw, at any rate he had a sudden flash of suspicion, and he sprang back and whipped out his pistol.

"Stand still!" he exclaimed in a low whisper; "don't move. Who the hell are you?" Kerrigan took off his hat and goggles. The Anglo-American stared at him. "What the blazes are you doing here?" he inquired after a pause.

"Heine was taken ill at the last moment," replied Kerrigan blandly, "and he asked me to deputise for him."

The Duke peered attentively at him and then remarked, with all his usual tranquillity:

"I don't understand it. And I'm afraid I haven't time to go into it now, which is a pity. The only possible assumption is that you're not the boob I took you for, and that seems incredible."

"Thank you," Kerrigan bowed.

"Anyhow," replied the other, picking up a length of rope, "I haven't time to go into that now. Turn round and put your hands behind your back. As I said before, I don't want to do you any harm:"

"I don't see how you can," replied Peter. "You see, your gun isn't loaded," and with that he hurled himself at the Duke, and for the second time within a quarter of an hour found himself engaged in a wrestling match. This time, also, it was an even match. Both men were wiry and immensely strong, and both appeared to know every trick, legitimate and illegitimate, of a public-house brawl or street-fight. After three minutes of desperate encounter they broke away and sprang to their feet, and the Anglo-American backed into a corner and emerged the next instant with a pair of knuckle-dusters on his hands. Kerrigan had slipped his off after felling Heine at the door of the Manor, and now, instead of hastily putting them on again, he held up his hand and said:

"Stop. I give in. I'm no boxer."

The Duke paused in his cat-like advance and said: "Straight?"

"Yes. Look here, I can't stop you getting away, and I'm no match for you. Why not just clear out and not worry about me? You're only wasting time. Even if I ran all the way to Bicester and told the police you'd be well away. They'll never catch you."

"There's something in that," said the Duke, "and time's getting short."

"And I give you my word of honour that I won't tell the police till tomorrow that you've gone in an aeroplane."

"Your word of honour be damned," replied the other, seizing the aeroplane. "You give me a hand in running her out into the field."

Five minutes later the last sound of the aeroplane's hum had died away in the darkness, and Peter Kerrigan sat down on the floor of the garage to examine the contents of the Anglo-American's pockets which he had scientifically picked, one by one, during their collision in the door of the Manor, their motor-bicycle journey in the darkness, and during their rough-and-tumble wrestling match.

XVII

The Treasure

It was after breakfast next morning before Kerrigan returned to Marsh Manor and found the whole place a seething mass of reporters, policemen, detectives, photographers, insurance-representatives (genuine ones), and, outside a cordon of police, sightseers with a very poor chance of seeing any sights.

Inspector Fleming took down the long depositions of everyone concerned, arrested Heine on a charge of being an accessory before the fact in the murders of John Hone, Rubin, Mr Tollemache, and the Colombian, warned Kerrigan that he might be arrested later on for the assault on Heine if that gentleman pressed the charge, and announced that he would advise the Chief Constable of the County to proceed against everyone, including Lady Caroline, for being in illegal possession of firearms.

After it was all over, Kerrigan at last was able to get hold of Lady Caroline.

"Well?" said the old lady with some asperity. "So he got away?"

"Yes. But I got the clue. And it looks to me like another cipher."

He handed her an envelope containing eleven sheets of yellow paper, closely written up in a queer crabbed handwriting.

Lady Caroline examined them with great care through her lorgnettes. At last she said slowly:

"I don't think this is in cipher. I'm going to London now. I want you to come with me."

"But the clue?" expostulated Kerrigan.

"Never mind about that," replied the old lady. "Go and get a motor-car."

XVIII

A Million Pounds

It was Heine who reluctantly cleared up a good many obscure points. Heine had been the Duke's chauffeur, gunman, and general mechanic for some years, and when the Duke got the commission from a newspaper-magnate in America, whose past had not always been so blameless as his present, to rid him of the blackmailing attentions of Mr Tollemache, art-valuer, art collector, and blackmailer, the two men with their attendant circus of satellites, removed themselves from Chicago to Europe to carry out the good work.

While in London, preparing to deal with the blackmailer, the Duke was approached with another offer of employment—this time by the agent of a Nebraska multi-millionaire whose conscience allowed him to do anything he liked. This employment consisted of extracting from a Mr John Hone the secret of a million-pound treasure about which he had spoken in certain discreet art-collecting circles.

The Duke, who was a quick worker, undertook this second job, and was agreeably surprised to find that the two overlapped. For after abducting Mr Tollemache one day from his house in Kensington, he discovered that he was at that very moment starting to blackmail Lord Claydon. Lord Claydon had, apparently, committed bigamy early in life, and was unwilling to go to prison, to see his son by his second wife disinherited, and to contemplate the prospect of his entire estates and fortune going, after his death, to the next heir who happened to be the half-caste son of a Jamaican cook. And it was in Lord Claydon's house that this million-pound fortune lay. It was almost too easy. Mr Tollemache's profession made him naturally a recluse into whose movements, appearances, and disappearances no one ever liked to inquire if even they had been interested, and his departure from the house at Kensington and rebirth at Marsh Manor passed unnoticed and un-discussed.

The first complication had been the appearance of Mr Rubin, acting on behalf of a North Dakota multi-millionaire. But Mr Rubin was not in the same street as a thief and a murderer as the Duke, and after he had, in a panic, killed the Duke's protégé and assistant, Newman, his fate was sealed.

Hone also had been kidnapped and had several times given, under pressure, partial and sometimes definitely incorrect information about the Treasure and the way to find it. In fact, the Duke's assistants at the house in St John's Wood had only just discovered the whereabouts of the packet of yellow papers under the boards in the bedroom which Hone had occupied at the Manor a few hours before the ex-librarian made his successful dash for liberty, which ended so fatally for him.

* * *

The Duke got clear away. His aeroplane was found in a field near Amsterdam, and a young man resembling him was seen boarding a train for Antwerp, but he was not heard of again until his reappearance on the north side in Chicago some months later.

Heine was hanged, and the remainder of the gang got long sentences. Lady Pamela married Streatfield. Lord Claydon and Sir George Ilford settled down to a quiet bachelor life at Marsh Manor.

The eleven yellow be-scribbled leaves of paper were unanimously declared by the experts to be part of Shakespeare's original manuscript of *Hamlet*, beginning: "Look here, upon this picture, and on this," down to "Lay not that flattering unction to your soul," and were sold in New York for the equivalent in dollars of one million two hundred and ten thousand pounds sterling. By mutual agreement Peter Kerrigan received two hundred and fifty thousand pounds, out of which he gave twenty thousand to the little Gower Street lecturer whose walk in the Euston Road had started it all.

The remainder, together with his hand and heart, he laid in a rash moment at the elegant feet of Rosemary Shackleford.

She considered the offer for a minute or two and then smiled and declined it. Peter was, on the whole, a little relieved, and they remained the best of friends.